JEEVES

A
Gentleman's
Personal Gentleman

To the Memory of
P. G. WODEHOUSE

JEEVES
A
Gentleman's
Personal Gentleman

C. NORTHCOTE PARKINSON

St. Martin's Press
New York

For information, write: St. Martin's Press,
175 Fifth Avenue, New York, N.Y. 10010
Manufactured in the United States of America

Designed by Paul Chevannes

Library of Congress Cataloging in Publication Data

Parkinson, Cyril Northcote, 1909-
    Jeeves.

        I.   Title.
PR6066.A6955J4   1981   823'.912   80-29160
ISBN 0-312-44144-4

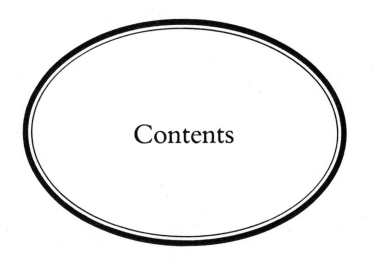

Contents

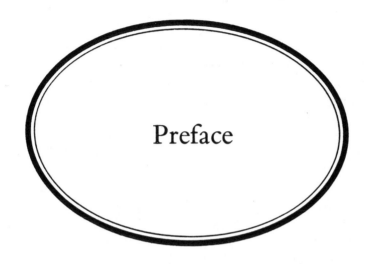

Preface

Biographies are, in general, books written about the Great and Good, occasionally about the Deplorable and Infamous. It is rare to find a published biography of someone still living whose life has been merely one typical of his country, period and class. A still greater rarity is a book of this description which can be said to merit careful study. Such a book is *Wooster's World* by Geoffrey Jaggard (London, 1967) in which the career of Mr Bertram Wilberforce Wooster is traced with the scholarly care of the sort usually lavished on former prime ministers, film stars, bishops and train robbers.

For the sake of the few who may not have read *Wooster's World* it should be emphasized at the outset that Mr Bertram Wooster is not, nor would claim to be, a celebrity in any way. He is simply a typical gentleman of his generation who went to Eton and Oxford, for which university he played racquets, and who divided the rest of his life between the West End of London and the country houses of his relatives and friends, ending up with a country house of his own. His habits have always been those of his friends, his addiction to nightclubs or to sport no greater than theirs. He has travelled, it is true, but merely to places regarded as fashionable at the time, as to Antibes or Hollywood. His means are ample, his friends influential, but he has had no ambition to achieve high office or greater wealth. His tastes are at least relatively simple and he has rarely moved outside the social circle into which he was born. His chief merit in the eyes of all who know him is his invariable loyalty to his friends and his eagerness to aid any of them in distress. The full extent of his kindness and generosity may never be known but it is something of which other people are at least vaguely aware.

If the work of the erudite Mr Jaggard falls thus into a rare category, the present work may be said to be unique. To trace Bertie Wooster's career can have been no easy task but his living relatives are numerous and their reminiscences bulk large. Wooster's name appears in many a footnote to many a published diary and some few incidents of his life are recorded in the newspaper clippings preserved by his more vindictive aunts. Some admirers, however, of Mr Jaggard's scholarship have been heard to remark that Wooster's career, of interest merely in being typical, is less worthy of record than would be the career of his former valet, Mr Reginald Jeeves. This suggestion, outrageous as it might at first appear, is not the outcome of communist influence but derives rather from the idea that Wooster owed a great deal to Jeeves's advice.

It seemed to the present author that there is substance in this theory. It is true, of course, that Jeeves was in the employ of various gentleman at various times. As against that, he would seem to have been a fount of wisdom to which all of Wooster's generation would turn in a crisis, Wooster himself included even when

Jeeves was valet or butler to someone else. The situation of the servant being wiser than his master is not unknown in literature – we think of Don Quixote and Sancho Panza, of Almaviva and Figaro – and may be known in life (even if examples of it do not so readily come to mind) and the idea seemed worth exploring. A very little research was enough to show that Jeeves was and is an abler man than all or most of his employers. So much was quickly evident. The author's difficulty lay in tracing the actual details of Jeeves's career; for the valet, however astute, leaves fewer traces than his master, however obtuse. There are no references to him in *Hansard*, no relevant paragraphs in *The Times*, no mention in the gossip columns. Our only authorities for the life of a servant must be the man himself, if still alive, and the reminiscences of the gentlemen by whom he was successively employed. For the recording of these recollections we rely in this modern age on the tape recorder, without which we could never have completed our story. The tape recorder has, however, its limitations. The most significant passages may be lost among other and irrelevant noises – grunts, snuffles and senile chuckles – and no tape, as we all know, is without a *gap* at its moment of greatest interest. Using these methods and overcoming these difficulties, some sort of narrative has been put together, lacking the structure of history but reflecting, we hope not inaccurately, a certain aspect of life.

It will occur to the reader to ask at this point why the author should make such heavy weather of what should be an easy task. Why was no sound receiver offered to Jeeves himself? Why do we not have the story as remembered by its central figure, a man whose memory might be expected to match his known intelligence? The answer is simple. Jeeves politely but firmly declined to be interviewed. He would not assist us in any way.

Why was this? Because he had kept a diary for the whole of his life and had every intention of basing upon it an autobiography which would be published at some future date. His should be a remarkable book when it appears and we can well understand its author's reluctance to connive at the theft of his own thunder. Having come up against this immovable obstacle many an author would have thought his task impossible. Why not give up the project and wait for Jeeves's own book to burst upon an astonished world? This would seem, at first sight, an unanswerable conclusion to have reached. There is, however, an objection to it that the reader, like the author, could not reasonably have foreseen. Jeeves will not write his autobiography until after he has retired, he will not retire until overtaken by old age and he shows every sign of outliving us all. Jeeves appears to be ageless, a person destined to attend discreetly the funeral of every character Mr Jaggard has had occasion to mention in his index, with the possible exception of Aunt Agatha. The result must be that his autobiography, fascinating as we may expect it to be, will come too late for all to whom it would be of the greatest interest, the author and his readers alike. For this reason the literary world is asked to accept, in the meanwhile, a second-best; the biography, in so far as we can piece it together, of a gentleman's personal gentleman.

C. Northcote Parkinson

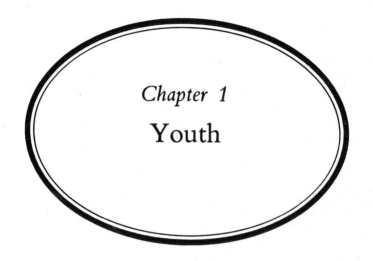

Chapter 1
Youth

With all false theories set aside, it is now clear as is the summer's sun that Reginald Jeeves was the only male offspring of Basil Jeeves and was therefore the grandson, beyond question, of the Rev. Theophilus Jeeves, the perpetually penniless Perpetual Curate of Pottering-up-Piddlecombe near Poole. Theophilus, being supposedly married, though we know not to whom, had numerous children and of these at least five survived their ill-nourished childhood. These were respectively named Mabel, Annie, Basil, Emily and Edith. Of the four daughters, Edith married Charles Silversmith, a brother of Tobias Silversmith, the jeweller of Hackney Wick who afterwards moved to Kensal Rise. The other daughters, plain beyond example, lived to become the three unmarried aunts: Mabel, insufferable from the day when her picture appeared as part of an advertisement for Wolkinshaw's Supreme Ointment; Annie, a martyr to swollen limbs who was detested by the other two; and Emily who was, sad to say, a devotee of the novels written by Rosie M. Banks.

In these circumstances we can scarcely wonder that the Rev. Theophilus Jeeves should have pinned all his hopes on Basil, who took no fewer than three prizes for scripture at Hogsnorton Grammar School. Nor was Theophilus initially disappointed, for young Basil went on to obtain a scholarship to Oriel College, Oxford, where he presently graduated with honours. Somewhat to his father's dismay, however, the young man declined to take holy orders and proposed rather to remain at Oxford as a lecturer in philology.

It should be explained at this point that a philologist is a student of language. Unlike many of his rivals in this subject, Basil devoted more attention to letters than to words, his first public lecture purporting to reveal, for the first time, the true origin of the letter P. His theory was well received but his academic future plainly depended upon its eagerly awaited sequel: a study (naturally) of the letter Q. Were that greeted with similar acclaim, he would undoubtedly obtain a fellowship at his own college. All depended, in short, on the success of his second appearance before the Philological Society. The assembled scholars all knew (as we all know, do we not?) that the Phoenicians had a sign, an emphatic voiceless velar, from which the Greeks derived their letter goppa. After using this for a few centuries the Greeks realized that this letter, even when voiced, could serve no purpose whatever since it merely duplicated the sound of their letter kappa or K. So they cleverly sold this redundant sign to the Romans who were too stupid to reject it. All this is common knowledge, but who first thought of improving the Q by the addition after it of U? Here was the problem which Basil set out to solve. Had he solved it? We shall never know. Not surprisingly nervous when the crucial day came, Basil accepted from his friends the stimulants which should have screwed up his courage to the sticking point. His had, however, been an abstemious life and what they gave him proved more, far more, than enough. He approached the rostrum in an alcoholic haze, shouted some nonsense about minding his p's and q's and ended prostrate on the floor. A believer, it would seem, in doing the job thoroughly, he shortly afterwards married Daisy Wiggins, the popular barmaid of the Cow and Crescent. He thus put a final period to what might have been a distinguished career.

Basil and Daisy moved to London at this point and it was there that Reginald, their only child, was born. For the rest of his life Basil was to make a scanty living as a proof-reader and index-compiler. We may picture him as eccentric, shabby, learned and normally drunk. One thing he always retained, however, would seem to have been a magnificent and pedantic command of the English language. When relatively sober, at least, his periods were rounded, his syntax perfect, his vocabulary extensive and his *mots* supremely *justes*. Daisy, who came from rural Oxfordshire, and who had no education at all, possessed the common sense which Basil so conspicuously lacked. She earned her living as a cleaner of the auditorium at Sadler's Wells but found time to cook occasional meals for her husband and child. Reginald in those days had some contact with Aunts Mabel, Annie and Emily and at least heard of his Uncle Charles, then a footman in Wimpole Street, but he owed his upbringing to his father. If Reginald went to school there is no record of it. We must rather suppose that life with Basil Jeeves, as he swayed over his proof sheets, was an education in itself.

Reginald was left an orphan by the age of fourteen but had gained by then a surprising gift for grammatical self-expression. His relatives sought to provide for his future by apprenticing him to Tobias Silversmith, but the latter reported after six months that the boy had no aptitude for the jeweller's craft. So Reginald was now attached, as hall boy, to the household of Mr Esmond Haddock of Deverill Hall, King's Deverill, in Hampshire; a household to which Charles Silversmith, Reginald's uncle-by-marriage, had recently been appointed as butler. He was from this time committed to a career as a domestic servant.

On hearing of this turn of events, the reader of today will utter, no doubt, a sigh of sympathy. How hard to be thrust so early into a life of ill-paid drudgery! Our minds may go back at this point to those maids-of-all-work or cooks-general we may have known in childhood. Very different, however, was the servant's life when this century began. Servants were then numerous enough to form a society of their own. Prosperous families moved between town and country houses, being often absent from both, leaving many of the servants to their own devices. At other times there were guests from whom tips were expected, and there was in any case a ladder of promotion from parlour maid to housekeeper, from nurserymaid to nannie, from footman to butler and from scullery maid to cook.

Young Reginald, known henceforward as Jeeves, could dream of eventually succeeding Mr Silversmith in office and he soon came to realize that a butler has perquisites as well as duties. In the meanwhile, his duties were far from onerous, his first task being to keep his uniform spotless, his second to carry logs for the fire, his third to pass a hot iron over each day's *Times* and *Morning Post*. While not actually running errands, he could watch the butler and note the way he would announce a visitor or reveal that dinner was served; and Silversmith set an example which any aspiring youngster did well to observe, mark, learn and inwardly digest.

No longer the slim footman of Wimpole Street, Charles Silversmith had become in middle age a figure to inspire both awe and dread. Weighing about sixteen stone, he moved with ponderous dignity about the Georgian rooms of Deverill Hall. Inimitable was his way of throwing open a double door. Portentous was his method of delivering a message. Terrifying was his look of disapproval, and the word abject is hardly strong enough to describe the attitude towards him of his underlings. In his presence even the older house guests were somewhat subdued and the younger guests were frankly petrified.* His wife Edith, Jeeves's aunt, was by comparison a dim figure in the background who scarcely spoke above a whisper and seldom emerged from the laundry of which she was administrative head. Silversmith himself spoke with a careful choice of words and was a leading exponent (as was the late Mr Gordon Harker) of the art of just not dropping an h. Jeeves's still more polished phrases he would have regarded as insolent had he ever heard them, but Jeeves in his presence never said more than, 'Yes, Mr Silversmith,' and, 'Very good, Mr Silversmith.' Nor did they ever sit at the same table, Silversmith taking his meals in the housekeeper's room and Jeeves being very properly relegated to the foot of the table in the servants' hall. He was, however, an observant lad and, saying nothing, listened well. He thus learnt that Esmond Haddock, JP, his bachelor employer, heir to a fortune made from Haddock's Headache Hokies, was much under the influence of his resident aunts, Daphne, Emmeline, Harriet and Myrtle. Of these the most obvious menace

---

* Silversmith is mentioned in *The Butlers of England* by Claude Manley but deserved more space than the author gave him. He is not to be compared, of course, with George Butterfield, whose memoirs are a classic of their kind, one in which Jeeves himself has merited a footnote reference. See *The Butler buttleth* (p. 94).

was Aunt Harriet, who continually urged her nephew to economize. If young Jeeves had not already learnt, as he had, to be wary of aunts, he would have learnt that lesson at Deverill Hall.

During his years as hall boy, Jeeves had every reason to regard Mr Silversmith with veneration but he was more influenced, in fact, by Mr Haddock's valet, Stephen Upnor. They first came briefly into contact when Huggins, the second footman, went down with appendicitis, Jeeves being detailed to take his place. Mr Upnor could hardly converse with a hall boy but might, just possibly, address a few words of advice to an acting footman. When he did so, he found in Jeeves an attentive listener.

'You should aim,' he said, 'at becoming a gentleman's personal gentleman. Why, you may ask. Because, I reply, that you go in that case where the master goes. If he is summoned to court, you must go too. Should he go to stay with the Duke of Surrey, he cannot go without his man. He will need his valet in the same way at Ascot, at Henley, at Cowes or in the Highlands, at Wiesbaden, Biarritz, Naples or Nice. There are those, no doubt, who are happy to stay all the year at Deverill Hall or Portman Place, but what life is that for a man of spirit? To see the world you must learn first how to press a suit, how to pack a portmanteau, how to hint gently that a collar is frayed. To be a valet you need a fund of knowledge, an observant eye, a talent for looking the other way and a gift, above all, of tact. You might have these talents, Jeeves, you could learn this art, and who with this prospect before him would be content to do nothing but lay the table and uncork the wine?'

Greatly impressed, Jeeves thanked Mr Upnor for his good advice and resolved some day to follow it.

Only two significant events broke the monotony of

Jeeves's life at Deverill Hall and both concerned Mr Haddock's Aunt Harriet, a tall angular woman with grey hair and a grating voice, the victim of many mysterious complaints which she readily described in detail to anyone foolish enough to ask her how she was. She specialized in headaches and shared them generously with her relatives. One day in late summer when the family and guests were having tea on the lawn, she complained at length about a sleepless night. Two lady guests expressed their sympathy but with that distant expression which was the prelude to moving away from her. Jeeves, told to make himself generally useful on these occasions, was within earshot, fetching rugs and moving deckchairs into or out of the shade. Having made a mental note of her complaint, he later came up to her and, with all due apologies for his temerity, offered her a packet of Haddock's Headache Hokies. He was at once transfixed by the mere flash of hatred in her eyes.

We all recall the scene when a messenger bounded up to Macbeth with the latest news, only to meet with the riposte, 'What bloody man is this?' We all have at least a general idea of what Jehovah thought about Sodom and Gomorrah, the cities of the plain. We could all picture the scene when Adolf Hitler was told about the Battle of Allemein, to which he reacted with a quick aside to ensure that the officer who conveyed the news should be shot. Neither Macbeth nor Hitler – nor even Jehovah – could have expressed more than a fraction of the loathing which Aunt Harriet now contrived to register.

'When I want your advice, Jeeves, I shall ask for it.' she said freezingly. 'Until then you will kindly hold your tongue.' She retired to her room with a renewed headache and Jeeves, panic-stricken, hid in the potting shed until the family had gone indoors. Later in the day he was summoned to appear before Mr Silversmith.

Looking at the butler's purple face and beetling brow, hearing the low rumble with which he cleared his throat (similar to, but harsher than, the MGM lion which heralds the motion picture) he gained the impression that he had forfeited all claim to popularity among the more senior members of the staff. A hedgehog in the throne room at Buckingham Palace could not have felt more friendless and alone.

'It has been brought to my notice, Jeeves, that you have been guilty of a serious breach of conduct. You are employed here in a humble capacity and you have duties which have been explained to you. A young man in your position is to be seen by the family on few occasions and not heard at all except in saying "Yes, sir" and "Very good, Madam," as the case may be. This is not a strict household, not nearly as strict as some I could name. In some great houses you would never be permitted to say "Very good, sir." Why not? Because the words might seem to convey an expression of opinion, as if in other circumstances you might have said "Very bad." But your master is a liberal-minded employer and believes in encouraging his staff to show initiative. You are thus free to say "very good" as an alternative to "yes". But you are *not* free to abuse that latitude. You must not regard "Very good, Madam," as the beginning of a conversation. If you have any comments to make you will make them silently. If you have views to express, remember that they are of no interest to anyone else. You are not paid (nor, in my opinion, overpaid) to think, talk or even pull faces. Your function is to appear immaculate, do as you are told and avoid notice at any time. When you enter a sitting room to make up the fire, the door should open and close silently, your footsteps should not be heard, the poker and tongs should make no clatter, and you should vanish as quietly as you came. Is that understood?'

'Yes, Mr Silversmith.' (in a whisper)

'You will now practise the art of silent movement and I shall expect you so to behave that we none of us know that you are in the house.'

'Yes, Mr Silversmith.' (barely audible)

'At the moment, Jeeves, your aunt and I are gravely disappointed in you, and the more so in that you were employed here on your aunt's recommendation. I shall hope to see a marked improvement in your behaviour.'

'Yes, Mr Silversmith.'

'You may go, Jeeves.'

The interview was over and the downcast Jeeves crept away to study the technique of ghost-like entry and silent evaporation. He was to become more than competent in this art but he wondered, in the meanwhile, what his real offence had been. For speaking out of turn he had deserved a rap over the knuckles, so much he knew, but how had he earned that look of pure hatred beneath which he had all but shrivelled? It was Mr Upnor who finally enlightened him.

'Well, Jeeves, you realize no doubt that the master's fortune comes from a patent medicine invented and marketed by his late father?'

'Yes, Mr Upnor.'

'What you have perhaps failed to grasp is that old Mr Haddock married Flora Deverill, the heiress to this estate, a daughter of the 7th Viscount Stockbridge.* The Deverills were appalled at the idea of a Deverill marrying a vendor of patent medicines. They utterly opposed the match, were all pointedly absent from the wedding and have never ceased to bewail this blot on their pedigree.'

* The Deverills were originally raised to the peerage by James II, but played little part in history. The 5th Viscount overslept on the day when he might otherwise have distinguished himself at the Battle of Inkerman.

'Yes, Mr Upnor?'

'Miss Harriet is the late Mrs Haddock's elder sister, unrelated (except by marriage) to Mr Haddock, and she bitterly resents even the most passing mention of the business from which his wealth derives.'

'I see, Mr Upnor. Should I apologize to her?'

'Are you out of your mind, Jeeves? Your apology would mean a further mention of Headache Hokies. Make yourself invisible and inaudible. Your trousers need pressing, your hair needs brushing. If you are ever seen, you must be fit to be seen.'

That concluded the first significant event in Jeeves's period of service at Deverill Hall. The second and last took place some two months later. He heard at that time a rumour that Mr Haddock had invested in a company called Barren Bogland Land Development of which Sir Jasper Todd was Chairman. When the Company went into voluntary liquidation Mr Haddock was thought to have lost some thousands of pounds, not enough to ruin him but enough to make him aggrieved and irritable. At Aunt Harriet's suggestion he now sent for Jeeves, she being present at the interview which ensued.

'Ah, Jeeves,' Mr Haddock began, 'there you are. I wanted to see you because – well, because some unforeseen circumstances make it imperative for me to curtail my household expenses. I propose to reduce my domestic staff by one.'

'Getting rid,' added Aunt Harriet, 'of the one who does least and is least likely to be missed.'

'I forget now what wages you earn—'

'Two shillings a week, sir.'

'Just so. That, with your uniform and keep, comes to—'

'At least £25 a year,' snapped Aunt Harriet.

'So, being forced to economize, I shall dispense with your services as from the end of the month. You are under notice, but I want to make it clear that you have not been found at fault.'

'Not been found out . . .' was his Aunt's muttered correction.

'So that I am able to give you a good reference. It so happens, moreover, that I can do more than that. Dame Daphne Winkworth, my aunt, widow of the well-known historian, is Principal of the Picklerod Academy for Young Ladies. She needs a new page-boy and I have told her that you would be not unsuitable. She is willing to have you on my recommendation.'

'And count yourself lucky to be employed at all!' With this parting shot Aunt Harriet left the room with a flourish and allowed her nephew to complete the transaction without further interruption. It was clear to her that his proposed economy would recover his loss in about a century and a half. As for Jeeves, he accepted his new appointment with some misgiving, aware as he was that experience at a girls' school would do little to prepare him for a career as a gentleman's personal gentleman. He realized, however, that there was no future for him at Deverill Hall while Aunt Harriet retained her influence there. He asked the advice of Mr Upnor, who assured him that he had no choice in the matter.

'As for Dame Winkworth,' he went on, 'I have seen her . . .' He shuddered for a moment and then continued: 'I have also heard of her Academy for Young Ladies. You should know from the outset that these Young Ladies are beyond parental control. Among those recently sent there is one known to have bitten her cousin in the leg, a second tried to poison a prize pig at Blandings Castle and a third set fire to the nursery wing at Long Smoldering Manor. Although coming from the best families, all pupils at Dame Winkworth's school are problem children. In your place I should refuse on principle to do anything they ask. On no account should you lend them any money.'

'That is easy,' said Jeeves, 'I have no money.'

'I suppose not,' replied Mr Upnor, 'Which gives you a good reason to refuse. You musn't, however, place their bets for them nor buy them cigarettes nor help them run away. But don't offend them neither or else they will tell Dame Winkworth that you have tried to kiss them in the shrubbery. Looking at your situation from every angle,' concluded Mr Upnor, 'it would be fair to say that you will need your wits about you.'

That this was a ludicrous understatement may not have been apparent at the time. It became obvious enough from the moment that Jeeves entered the great gates of Picklerod Academy, Starvely–Chillingworth, near Droitwich, and heard them close behind him with a resounding clang.

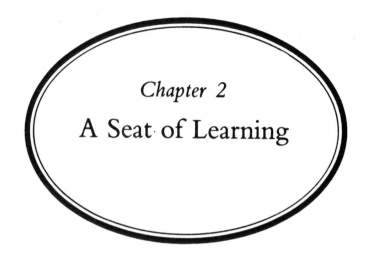

Chapter 2
A Seat of Learning

Picklerod Hall was built in 1887 for the late Mr Elisha Clutterbuck, who made his fortune from non-sulphurous iron ore. Alfred Waterhouse* was the architect and some there are who maintain that he was losing grip at this later period in his career. Be that as it may, Picklerod remains an impressive example of Victorian Gothic. In inspiration it wavers between the baronial and the monastic, nor is it without some trace of that lavatorial finish for which the University of Liverpool was so much admired in its heyday. It can boast a tower with gargoyles. It has ribbed vaulting and stained glass. It has castellated lodge gates and a high stone boundary wall. Whatever a gothic mansion should have Picklerod has: and has it moreover in profusion. Its first owner, Mr Clutterbuck, had no fewer

* Alfred Waterhouse (1830–1905), a distinguished architect who designed Salford Jail, Manchester, as also the National Liberal Club, and had his portrait painted by Alma Tadema.

than twenty-seven children by his three successive wives, successively worn out and tossed aside. His servants had been innumerable and so were the garret rooms to which they had been relegated. There is and has always been a striking contrast between the decor of the different floors. The entrance hall is thus remarkable for its mosaic tiles and moulded ceiling, still more for that mural depicting the Knights of the round table. Another mural, by the same artist and illustrating the quest for the holy grail, is a principal feature of the main staircase. Above the first floor, however, this artistic inspiration is quickly lost, its place being taken by dark brown paint and yellow varnished deal. If the ground floor rooms are somewhat ornate, the more utilitarian apartments are as conspicuously austere. The seekers of the holy grail might look upwards but they would certainly have never found it in the attic.

When Mr Clutterbuck died, his children, who had been a disappointment to him, migrated with alacrity to Capetown, Dunedin or Hobart, Picklerod Hall being eventually placed on the market. Times had changed, however, since 1887 and the demand for its gothic splendours was somewhat sluggish. It was on offer for some years, its price sagging as its murals faded, the scarlet turning to pink and the gilt to a mere brown. The market for troubadours and blessed damosels was not what it had been, gargoyles were at a discount and encaustic tiles were well below par. Dame Daphne Winkworth now acquired the property at a bargain price, perceiving that the vast structure was remote from all centres of population, sturdily built and well able to serve the essential purposes of a prison. When the rumour spread in Shropshire that the mansion was to become a home for difficult children, the neighbouring country folk all agreed that this was exactly what the place had always been. Where people were wrong was in using the word 'difficult' to describe girls who were mostly, in fact, impossible. Studying the building as it now stands, derelict, we have to admit that, whatever its drawbacks, it includes the essential requirements for a boarding school; an assembly hall, a chapel, a library, level ground on which to play hockey and a park from which escape was all but impossible.

Once the surly Hunkman had been installed at the lodge, Dame Daphne felt reasonably confident of keeping the girls in and keeping undesirable visitors out. Her own apartments overlooked the main entrance, no man slept on the premises and the porter, Hardrock, arrived each morning on his bicycle in time to ring the bell at seven o'clock. This was the signal for the girls to rise, wash, make their beds and tidy their attic rooms. At half-past seven the bell rang again for breakfast and at eight the girls went to morning prayers and so to class at eight-thirty. It might be supposed that a Gauleiter like Dame Daphne would have recruited an academic staff which shared her gift for inspiring terror, but that had never been her policy. Her preference had been for the diffident and downtrodden, for women whose services had often been dispensed with and whose resignation from Picklerod would have been the prelude to a long period of unemployment. Few of them were mentally negligible but none was capable of answering back. If there was an exception to this rule it would have been Miss Wuthering, Second Mistress, who was the Principal's second cousin, but her display of independence was no more, at most, than an annual event.

When the outer gates shut behind Jeeves, he was shown to his upstairs room in the lodge, furnished with iron bedstead, flock mattress, washstand and basin. When he reported for duty at the back entrance of the main building, Mr Hardrock told him what his duties would be. After taking the morning's newspapers to the

Principal's apartment and the common room, he might breakfast with the other servants and tidy up the top floor. Any clothes or books left lying about he was to gather up and deliver to Room 13, from which they could be recovered on payment of a fine. At nine he would collect the letters for post and take them to the pillar-box outside the main gate. At nine-thirty he would report to the Principal . . . and so his day was organized from hour to hour until the last bell sounded for lights out at ten.

'All that,' explained the elderly and spectacled Mr Hardrock, 'is simple enough. But you must also learn how to deal with the girls. Some are spoilt and will order you about. Take no notice of 'em. Others will try to make friends with you. These are the ones to be wary of. Tell 'em you have your own work to do – as you have, to be sure. Then there are the girls with red hair – don't trust 'em for an instant and don't let 'em catch you alone.'

'What happened to the last page-boy?'

'He had to leave rather suddenly and without a character. The girls complained to the Principal that he tried to kiss them.'

'In the shrubbery?'

'No, that was another page-boy, the last but two. We seldom seem to keep 'em for long.'

'It seems to me, Mr Hardrock, that a boys' school would be a great deal easier.'

'So it would in some ways, Jeeves, and I'll tell you why. With boys you know, more or less, what they are thinking. If they are not paying attention, you can see that they are in a dream about something else. If they are lying they most often stammer and blush. But a girl who seems attentive may not have listened to a blessed word you've said and a girl who is lying will look you straight in the eye.'

'Are any of them specially dangerous?'

'It would be quicker to list the few that aren't. But the worst mischief maker is Sally Phipps-Gunning. Kate Medlingham is almost as bad with Susan Gatling no better and Dinah Billinghurst seemingly worse.'

'Are any of those red-haired?'

'They are all red-haired, and so is Margaret Drover and Jane Mottisham. Cunning they are, some of 'em. But they know better than to try their tricks on me!'

The daily time-table allowed about fifteen minutes between morning assembly and the first period of work, time available for fetching books and washing hands. It was during this pause for thought that Jeeves was accosted one day by a young fair-haired girl called Brenda Bunting. She was breathless from having pelted down the upper stairs but her message was clear enough. A bird had flown into her attic room and was unable to find its way out. It was dashing itself against the window panes and the room was being covered with feathers and dirt. Would Jeeves come to the rescue? After three weeks at Picklerod, Jeeves regarded all the girls with dark suspicion. But Brenda was small, innocent and tearful, and had no background of crime. He felt like any cavalier might have felt in going to aid a damsel in distress. Had there been fewer people about, they would probably have run upstairs hand-in-hand. Unhindered, however, by any such sentimentality they reached the top floor in what might have been record time. Brenda led Jeeves to Room 66 and gazed at him admiringly as he threw the door open and entered. A second later the door slammed behind him and he heard the key turn in the lock. There was no bird in the room and no sign that any bird had ever been there. He had been fooled! And what would Dame Daphne say if it transpired that he had been found in Brenda's bedroom? Jeeves remembered, however, that the dormer windows of these attic rooms opened on a parapet which offered the usual means by which the girls raided each other. He strode to the window, which opened helpfully at that moment to reveal the kind face of a brunette called Jill Sempill.

'You poor dear!' She cooed, 'What a rotten trick to play on you! Never mind, you can escape this way. Come to mother!'

While opening the casement to its full extent, Jill herself blocked the way. Jeeves hesitated, knowing that he had to be on duty in five minutes.

'Please, Miss—' he began.

'But I want a tiny reward for letting you out. Just one little kiss . . . agreed?'

'Yes, Miss – with pleasure, Miss!' She moved aside and he was out of the window in a flash. Then her arms were round him and her mouth on his.

'Hold it!' said another girl's voice. There was a significant click and she added 'That's fine!'

Breaking free, Jeeves saw that three other girls were gathered round, the one with the camera being the red-haired Sally Phipps-Gunning. The other two, on the other side of him were holding wine glasses which were being filled from a bottle. The snap just taken would record something more than a casual kiss. It would be a memento of a roof-top orgy, a night on the tiles. He thought for an instant of snatching the camera but Sally had foreseen that move, retreating promptly with Jill as rearguard. He had no time, anyway, for any such skirmish. Climbing quickly through the window of the next room, he found the door open and ran downstairs again amid the giggles of all the girls he passed. Half of them must have known exactly what had happened and all the rest would be told during the mid-morning break. He was on the ground floor, nevertheless, before his absence had been noticed. Cursing himself, he thought how easily he had been trapped.

These bitches had probably done it all before. That was probably how they planned the dismissal of his predecessor. But would they complain to the Principal immediately? On the whole, he thought not. Their game, he thought, was blackmail. He would know soon enough what he would have to pay for their silence.

A week later he was intercepted in the entrance hall by Sally Phipps-Gunning. After glancing round to see that nobody was within earshot, she said quietly: 'Hello, Jeeves. That photograph has turned out rather well. I thought you would like to see the print.' She pulled it out from the flyleaf of an algebra textbook. 'A good likeness of you, we thought. We have given it the title "Thanks for the memory". The other prints and the negative are hidden, but NOT in my room.' She paused for a moment and Jeeves realized, not for the first time, that she was wildly pretty. Her next words had no apparent connection with what she had been saying. 'Susan and I, Kate and one or two of my friends are a bit tired of cleaning our shoes. There are six of us all told. We thought you would like to do them after supper.' She looked at him brightly and then added, with an air of generosity: 'We'll put them outside our doors – and, yes, we'll provide the boot polish.'

'Very good, Miss.' What else could he say? He was to clean and polish their shoes for many weeks to come. But that was only the beginning, for Sally and her friends had other tasks for him, some quite as menial and others increasingly dangerous. As for Brenda Bunting, who had originally led him into the trap, she now passed him in the corridor without so much as glancing in his direction. It was quite obvious that she had never seen him before. Jill Sempill made no such pretence, winking at him so as to make her friends giggle.

In the background to this drama there loomed the

figure of Dame Daphne Winkworth.* She figures in
many a book of memoirs and is described by all her old
pupils with a shudder. Few of them have much to say
about her severity and it does not appear that her regime
was really so harsh. She seems to have imposed her will
by sheer force of personality, now addressing the
assembled girls with a wealth of sarcasm but more often
merely staring at them with disapproval. She was tall,
grey-haired and eagle-nosed, her steel rimmed spectacles flashed as she strode the corridors, her eyes darted
round for signs of dirt and disorder, her voice was loud
and her manner Napoleonic. She was like a fast ocean
liner which leaves all lesser craft tossing in her wake.
Jeeves stood aside when he saw her approach and would
shudder at the prospect of facing her wrath. One or two
small errors he had already made with shattering sequel.
The effect on her of that photograph, were she ever to
see it, would simply not bear thinking about.

The crisis came towards the end of that first term.
Sally Phipps-Gunning waylaid Jeeves in the passage
behind the scullery.

'Ah, there you are, Jeeves; the very young man I
wanted to see. Some friends of mine are planning a
party, a sort of farewell to Susan, whose last term this is.
We shall want some cigarettes and a bottle of port.' She
produced a ten shilling note. 'I know you can arrange it.
By tomorrow, please.'

'But look, miss, this is too risky altogether. I can't do
it.'

Jeeves fully expected a reminder, at this point, that he

---

* See *Great Women Teachers of the Victorian Age* by Harriet Hairbun. Unfortunately for Dame Daphne's subsequent fame, the names in this standard
work are taken in alphabetical order, giving Miss Beale and Miss Buss an
unfair advantage over anyone whose name begins with W. Dame Daphne
merits no less than four pages but hers is the last name in the book and few
readers, if any, have read so far.

faced dismissal if he refused. But Sally did not threaten him on this occasion. She strolled with him a few yards until they came into the open air. Her red-gold hair was light in the sunlight, her warm brown eyes were affectionate and gentle, her wringable neck was gracefully rounded, her skin was heart-breakingly white and her whole manner was completely changed. She kissed him very deliberately on the mouth and said in a whisper, 'You will do this, won't you – for me?'

He replied, 'Yes, miss,' before he knew what he was saying. What other reply was possible? A few minutes later he was sitting on the backstairs in deepest dejection, and that is where Miss Harbottle found him.

Miss Eunice Harbottle, BA (Hons.) taught English Literature up to sixth form level and can be said to have taught it rather well. She was middle-aged and spectacled with a pink nose and a permanent sniff as a result of sinus trouble. She was no disciplinarian and the girls jeered at her as a frustrated spinster, dowdily dressed. But the sight of Jeeves awoke in her a maternal instinct for which she had normally insufficient scope.

'By the waters of Babylon I sat down and wept,' she sighed. 'Tell me, Jeeves, what your trouble is.' He needed little persuasion and in a very few minutes had told her all.

'I see – another of Sally's tricks! I know that young lady of old. I also know one or two things about her which she wouldn't like Dame Daphne to hear about. "She was a vixen when she went to school . . ." (*A Midsummer Night's Dream*). Leave this with me, Jeeves, and do nothing more for Sally or her friends.'

Jeeves followed this advice and was accosted again, two days later, by Sally, whose looks (as Miss Harbottle would have remarked) now bore a terrible aspect.

'I have some photographs for you,' she said stiffly, 'and the negative.' After handing them over, she went on: 'We decided not to hold that party after all. We think, by the way, that you are a nasty sneaking, squeaking pink-eyed rat.'

So ended what might have been a beautiful friendship and began Jeeves's new life under the tutelage of Miss Harbottle. She had decided to give him the education he had so far lacked, and he could easily have had a far worse teacher. She had a genuine love of literature and found in Jeeves a more responsive pupil than most of the girls she was paid to instruct. Although she made Jeeves begin reading at once, her real opportunity, and his, began with the end of term.

Once the girls had gone, Dame Daphne went to her villa in the south of France, some of the other teachers went home or travelled on package tours to Italy. Miss Wuthering took over the Principal's office and dealt with her correspondence, assisted by Miss Harbottle, who had nowhere to go. The domestic staff settled down to an easy routine of maintenance and gossip. As for Jeeves, he was given the run of the library, together with a reading list and notebook. He was to begin each day with Shakespeare or Milton but might relax in the afternoons with Kipling or Keats. Browsing on his own, he came across Spinosa and Nietzsche and dabbled in Philosophy. He owed to his father a gift for spoken English and to this he now added a wide and widening knowledge of literature, with a few Latin tags for decoration.

Miss Harbottle may have had some vague idea that he would eventually pass examinations but she soon realized that he lacked that sort of ambition. His object, he explained, was to become a gentleman's gentleman. In that way, he explained, he would go to all the more fashionable resorts at other people's expense. In no other way could he travel for nothing and be paid for his time. Accepting the truth of this theory, Miss Harbottle suggested to him that a valet with a knowledge of literature would be all the more valuable to any gentleman of intellect, scholarship and culture. That she was right is beyond question but Jeeves, as we shall see, was to have few employers of that calibre. It is true, nevertheless, that his gifts and knowledge were to earn him respect throughout his career. All this he owed to Miss Harbottle, without whose encouragement he could never have used the school library on all those holidays, spread as they were over nearly three years. Of many another man it could be said,

> *Sir, he hath never fed of the dainties that are bred in a*
>   *book;*
> *he hath not eat paper, as it were; he hath not drunk*
> *ink: his intellect is not replenish'd; he is only an*
> *animal, only sensible in the duller parts:*
>   *(Love's Labour's Lost,* Act IV Scene II)

but this could never henceforth be said of Jeeves. Given his retentive memory, he was to end as a man of parts, ready to quote from the classics and far from ignorant of contemporary drama and fiction.

When the girls returned at the beginning of term Jeeves was once more the witness of their revolting behaviour. He was no longer the victim of any plot for the word had gone round that he was in a position to blackmail the leading rebel, but he came to know what mischief was being planned by whom. With Miss Harbottle's help, moreover, he became familiar with *Debrett* and *Who's Who,* concluding that many of the girls came from families in which the most appalling conduct would pass as normal. If Kate Medlingham was a pest, it was at least relevant to know that she was descended from an illegitimate son of George IV. If Jane Mottisham was a nuisance it was not altogether surprising, her mother being the great great grand-daughter of Lord Spendlove. One girl's grandmother had been a Gaiety Girl, another child's mother, who died early of pneumonia, had been in the chorus at the Windmill. The father of one had been cashiered from the Lifeguards for cheating at the bridge table, the grandfather of another had been court-martialled for being drunk before, during and after the Battle of Jutland. When Helena Nutshell wrote naughty words on the bathroom ceiling, Dame Daphne was heard to mutter, 'But all that family were always mental.'

When Deirdre Dotterell put a chamber pot in a position where it could not possibly be of any use, Miss Harbottle said to Miss Wuthering: 'What else can we expect? An ancestor of hers was a fully-paid-up life member of the Hellfire Club.'

In after years, looking back on this period of his life, Jeeves used to reflect that Dame Daphne might have done better to ensure that her pupils were more fully occupied when not actually in class. Her chief and undeniable success was in preventing their escape but there was little to prevent them raising hell within the boundary walls. Hell, accordingly, was what they raised and in such various forms as to fill the onlooker with pity and terror. The devil, it is said, finds work for idle hands to do. In its great days Picklerod Academy must have left him with precious little time for anything else.

Events which Jeeves was to remember included the fire alarm which was started by the planting of a smoke grenade (stolen from someone's elder brother in the Brigade); the laying of the false scent which led the local pack to race at full cry through the central corridor and out through the staff commonroom; the unexpected visitor – a Countess, seemingly, with a grand-daughter to educate – who turned out to be one of the girls in disguise; the boys seen in the dormitory whose presence there led to a full-scale inquiry but whose shorts and blazers were afterwards found in a cupboard; the gaming saloon established in what had been the wine cellars, and Miss Pearson's discovery of the roulette board; the beer-brewing plant set up in the disused harness room; and the protection racket which deprived the new girls of their pocket money.

Stories have been written, published and televised about the escape plans made by British officers held prisoner in the maximum security prison of Colditz. Not even the few who actually escaped could have had much to teach the girls of Picklerod Academy. Escape was seldom the girls' object, of course, but they were in their way as ingenious, as heartless and (when questioned) as dumb as any Colditz hero could ever have been. Being sent to the Academy as nuisances in the home, they improved their techniques by the swapping of information under the leadership of those whose criminal record was the worst. It is doubtful whether the full story of Picklerod will ever be told but there would be material enough for a thirteen-part television series with a musical theme by Robert Farnon.

Thinking about all the escapades which had come to his knowledge, Jeeves shuddered to think that these revolting specimens of girlhood would some day marry and produce yet others of their like. Some wretched man would marry Susan Gatley, another would be snared by the innocent looks of Brenda Bunting, a third poor simpleton might walk up the aisle with Sally Phipps-Gunning herself. What a hard fate would these bachelor men bring on themselves! But that is not where the sad story would end. For these women would not be childless. In the words of Macbeth:

What, will the line stretch out to th' crack of doom?—
Another yet? – A seventh? – I'll see no more:—

And yet the eighth appears, who bears a glass
Which shows me many more . . .
Horrible sight;   (He could say that again)

It was at this stage in his life that young Jeeves decided against marriage altogether. It was a bachelor he would remain, as a gentleman's personal gentleman ought to be. Many a youngster makes this resolve, only to find it evaporate in the presence of some girl he thinks adorable. But few young men have been educated, as was Jeeves, in a girls school, and fewer still in Picklerod Academy for Young Ladies. Did ever a Picklerod page-boy appear as proud progenitor? We doubt it. If the f of the species is deadlier than the m this is a lesson which Jeeves learnt well under the auspices (whatever they may be) of Dame Daphne Winkworth. He was not wholly averse to flirtation and he was later to be seen, though rarely, on the dance floor. But wild horses could not have dragged him to the altar and there is no record, indeed, of these animals having even made the attempt.

For information about Jeeves's early life we must rely mainly on his own reminiscences* but we have another and valuable source in the unpublished memoirs of Miss Harbottle. Throughout her teaching career she kept a record of her uninteresting life and this she finally deposited in the Silverfish Library at Detroit. It is clear from this manuscript that Jeeves made a great impression on her and that she followed his subsequent career with interest. Her motive in writing was to say on paper all she thought about Dame Daphne and would never have dared say to that lady's face. Considered as an exercise in vituperation her work has thus a certain claim on our

---

* The reminiscences, that is to say, which he has revealed from time to time in casual conversation. We have nothing from him (Vide supra, p. 9) in writing.

attention. The pity is that she wrote so little about Jeeves.

She does describe, however, the circumstances in which he left the school, dismissed it is true but through no fault of his own. By her account, which we must surely accept, he owed his downfall to the Hon. Sylvia Soleful, a new girl in what was to prove his last term. She was no hell-raiser but merely a girl who yearned for male affection, something which had no place in the Academy's Prospectus. Aroused (and she was all too easily aroused) by her reading of *Romeo and Juliet*, she cast poor Jeeves in a role for which he was singularly under-rehearsed. He was not particularly flattered by her expressed preference – there was, after all, no other male under sixty within her orbit – and he certainly did nothing to encourage her. Who was Sylvia, he asked himself, and what was she that all the swains should adore her? In truth she was nothing out of the ordinary and could have leaned on a balcony for a long time before anyone responded to the challenge. Far from monopolizing attention, she was a plain girl who had never had enough. When Jeeves failed to respond in any way, Sylvia revealed all in letters addressed to her elder sister; letters which were promptly shown to her mother. That it was a one-sided friendship was sufficiently apparent but Dame Daphne, when informed, thought proper to end it. She sent for Jeeves and told him that his successor had been appointed. He himself had not been at fault but Lord Worplesdon, Chairman of the School's Board of Governors, had a vacancy, she had heard, for a second footman. Jeeves was to leave in the morning and report to Lord Worplesdon at once.

'If it were done,' replied Jeeves, '—when 't's done 'twere well it were done quickly . . .'

Dame Daphne looked startled at this, failing to see that she had been cast in the role of Lady Macbeth, but recovered quickly enough to hand him his wages and a letter of recommendation. Then he went to say goodbye to Miss Harbottle, who was close to tears. Thanking her for all her kindness in the past, he told her that to become a second footman was promotion and a step he dared not refuse.

'Beware,' she replied, 'of vaulting ambition, which o'erleaps itself, and falls on the other.'

He said that he would avoid that mistake, he really would. She hoped that he had learnt something from his years at Picklerod. He said that he had, he really had, and this was no more than the truth.

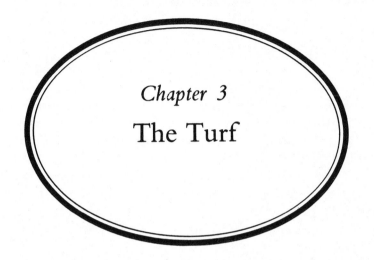

Chapter 3

The Turf

The Rt. Hon. the Earl of Worplesdon's country house was at Worpley Maltravers, his town house in Curzon Street, his office in Southampton but his heart in Newmarket. In the world of commerce he was known as the Chairman and principal owner of the Pink Funnel Line, trading to Argentina and Brazil. A valuable part of this trade was in shipping dirty linen from Buenos Aires to London, and the same linen, when laundered and ironed, back to the Argentine where men of wealth had no laundry facilities which would be judged adequate for a man of fashion. Ships of the Pink Funnel Line all have names like Pink Azalea, Pink Star, Pink Sunset, Pink Elephant or Pink Panther. The Line was founded by Daniel Craye, a merchant seaman of note, and his grandson, the present Earl, spent some time at sea after leaving Oxford. There followed the maritime disaster in which the 2nd Earl perished, together with his elder son, Lord Maltravers; a catastrophe in which two ships of the Pink Funnel Line collided with each other off the

Isle of Wight. Both vessels sank immediately, both were heavily insured and neither had recently been trading at a profit.

So the 3rd Earl, as Percival Craye, the younger son, now became, inherited a fortune which was no longer tied up in shipping. He closed his country house, moved to Curzon Street, and began what some would describe as a life of dissipation. That might, in fact, be too strong a word but he was much in evidence in the West End for a number of years, no big social event being complete without him. He presently announced his engagement to Agatha Wooster, who had been the most formidable debutante of what must have been a vintage year. The match was approved by the two families concerned and photographs appeared in all the society periodicals. Understandably apprehensive about the marriage to which he was now committed, Percival made vigorous use of the period of freedom which remained to him, going so far as to take Tottie Lushington to a ball at Covent Garden. What actually happened there has passed into a legend and is the subject of many a whispered reminiscence, but the upshot was that he and Tottie were thrown out and taken to Vine Street Police Station. This event and their subsequent appearance in court had ample press coverage and the clippings were enough to end the 3rd Earl's engagement. He was rarely seen in the night clubs as from this time and he took up what was to be his normal residence at Worpley Maltravers. He also reappeared in the world of shipping, and the Pink Funnel Line entered upon a new phase of prosperity under his guidance, one which led eventually to the merger with Latin American Coasters Ltd. He married later and had issue but his wife died at a relatively early age and he was for some years a widower, the elusive target for many a maternal plot.

It is a strange and paradoxical facet of human nature

that men whose careers are tied to the land should be chiefly interested in sailing whereas those whose lives are wedded to the deep are mainly interested in horses. It is thus a well-known fact of biology that the winner of practically every yacht race turns out to be a lieutenant-colonel and that any naval officer who may compete is lucky to come in seventh on handicap. As against that, naval officers predominate on the polo field and are to be found on every racecourse with their Admiralty-pattern binoculars at the ready. It was Vice Admiral the Hon. H. J. Rous who dominated the Jockey Club during Queen Victoria's reign and it was he, as we all know, who drew up the Scale of Weight for Age.

In much the same way the 3rd Earl's real interest was not in cargo vessels so much as in flat racing. He had a place, Saddlesope Lodge, near Newmarket, and owned at one time a half share in a filly called Dainty Lass, winner of the Oaks. But his enthusiasm for the sport was not enough in itself to ensure his success. The horses he owned were apt to go down with glanders, the horses he backed were rarely even placed. He was Chairman, as we have seen, of the Governors of Picklerod Academy and it is the sad fact that at least a dozen of the girls incarcerated there could have placed his bets for him with a far greater measure of success. That he never asked their advice is understandable – for no sporting news was supposed ever to pass its cas-tellated gate – but even his own domestic staff did better on the turf than he did. Bugsley, the butler, lost money admittedly, but this was through following his master's lead through a mistaken notion of loyalty. Formright the first footman, did well. Gunn the gamekeeper did better still and Vaisey the valet did best of all. That Vaisey should often spot the winner is understandable because he, unlike the others, went with the Earl to Newmarket and so had ready access to the racing stables or at least to the public houses where the odds were bandied about. Vaisey made it a rule in betting to do the converse of what his employer had decided to do, a practice which saved him from many a costly blunder. Vaisey never gave hot tips to his fellow servants, however, saying that careless talk might shorten the odds.

Coming into this household, Jeeves began what was to be the work of a lifetime; the study of form. He had, as Miss Harbottle had discovered, an exceptionally retentive memory. He had made himself familiar with *Debrett* and had traced the lines of hereditary eccentricity which accounted for at least some of the events which took place in his time at Picklerod Hall. In arguments about the relative importance of heredity and environment he was never in doubt as to his own opinion, based as it was on years of sad experience. He now passed from human beings to horses, reading all the textbooks, following the racing news and listening carefully to all the gossip. His knowledge was encyclopaedic before he so much as placed a bet of his own. That Jeeves knew his subject backwards was generally recognized, and the day came when he was actually called in to settle a dispute between two of Lord Worplesdon's horsiest friends, the Hon. Mark Cannonbone-Fetlock and General Hackenham-Heltoyou.

'Look, Jeeves, we have been talking about Hyperion and of why so little was expected of him at first. The General here thinks that he stood only fifteen hands but I can't believe that. I stand to lose my bet if he is right.'

Your money is safe, sir, and I can assure the General that he has been misinformed – although, to be sure, I have heard that said about Hyperion before. He stood fifteen hands and one and a half inches on the day he won the Derby.'

'Dammit!' growled the General, 'I must take your word for it. But there was a prejudice against him, perhaps for some other reason.'

'Yes, sir, he had four white socks and there used to be a superstition about it. Punters would have done better to recall that he was descended through Eclipse from the Darley Arabian. Bay Ronald was his great-grandsire so that he was in the male line from Touchstone. By Gainsbrough out of Selene, his dam line was one of the best in the stud book. He descended indeed from Old Bald Peg, the No. 6 foundation mare.'

'What, do you believe in Mr Bruce Lowe's classification?'

'No, General. It is no longer upheld, but Hyperion's ancestry would be difficult to better and it has been shown since by the number of winners he has sired. But I think we should also give some credit to Mr George Lambton, his trainer, and Tommy Weston, the jockey. He might have won the Derby in any case but we should recall that he won it by four lengths and in a record for the course of two minutes and thirty-four seconds. As Shakespeare says—'

'Was *he* a betting man?' asked the Hon. Mark Cannonbone-Fetlock with a look of surprise.

'I fancy so, sir, as witness his words:

> *"Round-hoofed, short jointed, fetlocks shag and long*
> *Broad breast, full eye, small head and nostril wide,*
> *High crest, short ears, straight legs, and passing strong,*
> *Thin mane, thick tail, broad buttocks, tender hide."* '

'Good grief!' said the General, 'I had always thought of Shakespeare as a hurdle in the School Certificate – a sort of Beecher's Brook.'

'He had an eye for a horse, General. You may recall, sir, his contrasting description of a probable loser:

> "... *Possess'd with the glanders, and like to more in the chine; troubled with the lampass, infected with the fashions, full of windgalls, sped with spavins, ray'd with the yellows, past cure of the fives, stark spoil'd with the staggers, begnawn with the bots; sway'd in the back, and shoulder-shotten; ...*"

you will find the passage in *The Taming of the Shrew*, Act III, Scene II. In his former description of a likely winner he should perhaps have specified that the animal should be able to convert lactic acid into muscle sugar while at the gallop but he might have found that difficult to rhyme or scan. Will that be all, sir?'

Lord Worplesdon's relatives included an uncle called the Hon. Derek Craye, younger brother of the 2nd Earl, an elderly gentleman of no fixed abode who might be desribed as a professional guest. His year was planned as a circuit, passing from one country house to another. A bedsitting room in Ebury Street was his only address and that is where he kept his wardrobe, repacking there so as to be suitably dressed for the time of year. He had lived extravagantly in early life and now had paid the penalty, being detailed to read to the bedridden, push the wheelchair or take the children to the pantomime. His visits to Worpley Maltravers were usually timed to coincide with some sporting event which would take the Earl elsewhere, as it might be to Goodwood or Ascot. The 3rd Earl was notoriously short-tempered at breakfast and was apt to regard his uncle with a baleful stare which Derek found unnerving. Expressing his surprise and regret on each occasion, he would hail the Earl's departure with inward relief, stay for a quiet fortnight or so and would usually have gone before his Lordship's return. After the pattern of Uncle Derek's life had been explained to him, Jeeves offered to act as valet to this particular guest.

'You must be crazy,' replied the butler with scorn. 'That old meal snatcher never gives more than a shilling to anyone.'

'It will be good practice all the same,' said Jeeves and he proceeded to acquire, second-hand, the sort of dark suit which Vaisey usually wore. When Uncle Derek arrived and was shown to one of the smaller guest rooms, the one which overlooked the kennels, Jeeves reported for duty and offered to unpack for him.

'But who are you?' asked Derek. 'I've only seen you as footman, passing round the brussel sprouts.'

'I am to act as your valet, sir, when Mr Bugsley can spare me.'

'And so be ready to take Vaisey's place after he has made his fortune on the turf. Tell me, do you know anything about a valet's job?'

'I am quick to learn, sir.'

'And I can teach you, but it's I who will expect the tip at the end of my visit.'

'Very good, sir. Shall I unpack for you now?'

'No, you can watch me this time. I learnt from my own valet in the days when I could afford one and he, I can tell you, was no amateur. Now, the secret is to do things in the right order . . .'

By the time of Uncle Derek's second visit, Jeeves had managed to secure for him one of the better guest rooms while his mentor had brought with him a second portmanteau and a wider selection of clothes, some appropriate for playing polo at Hurlingham and others fit to appear on the Squadron Lawn at Cowes. On his third visit Uncle Derek had a third portmanteau containing the mess uniform and blue patrols, the mess wellingtons and spurs he had once worn in the Royal Dragoons, the tropical kit he had worn when attending a Durbar in New Delhi, the court dress which would be essential to one about to receive the honour of knighthood and the tweeds which a guest might suitably wear during a weekend at Balmoral. Once he had learnt how to pack and unpack, how to sponge and iron every conceivable garment a gentleman might wear, Jeeves was then handed a number of volumes from which he learnt the Order of Precedence, the sequence in which orders and medals are displayed and the significance of the ties worn, whether associated with school, college, regiment or club. Uncle Derek was no pedant, however, and he thought that a valet needed to know little more than the elements of heraldry and the tartans of but a dozen of the principal highland clans. He was eloquent, however, on the term 'a gentleman's gentleman' which was applied, as Jeeves knew, to the well established valets of this world.

'In earlier days,' he explained, 'a king used to be waited upon by nobles, a Duke to hand him his breakfast tray, a mere Marquis to empty his chamber pot. Each noble was similarly attended by gentry, an Esquire to hold his horse, a page to light his candle. And even a prosperous gentleman might have a less prosperous gentleman, as his personal attendant. This is no longer the custom but the tradition lingers to some extent. It is proper to hear a head groom speak with a Yorkshire accent, a head gardener with a Scottish brogue, and a gamekeeper in some dialect learnt from the works of D. H. Lawrence. But a valet, a gentleman's gentleman, should speak the King's (or Queen's) English, and I am glad to think that you could do that before ever you learnt to remove a soup stain from a white waistcoat. I foresee for you, Jeeves, a distinguished career, with even the royal household not far beyond your grasp.'

On Uncle Derek's fourth visit Jeeves was to learn that a valet must also know how to cook. He need not be able to serve a seven course dinner or even a particularly formal luncheon but his preparation of breakfast must be impeccable and a supper fit for a bachelor's table should not be beyond his skill. Nor should he be ignorant of whisky, gin, sherry or the main types of apéritif, for the occasion may arise when there is no butler at hand: as there are bachelor establishments indeed where no butler is ever seen. Jeeves was quick to learn all that he needed to know, whether about cooking omelettes or about the decanting of port, and the time came when he could be said to have surpassed his teacher. His period of instruction ended soon after Uncle Derek's attempt to show him how bacon and eggs are cooked to perfection. The demonstration was disastrous but the more serious trouble was that it involved an invasion of the kitchen, which the Chef bitterly resented. He complained to Lord Worplesdon after that nobleman's return and a decision was then taken that Derek Craye should never be invited to Worpley Maltravers again. This seriously disrupted the pattern of Derek's annual circuit, compelling him to stay for an extra week at Ickenham Hall, ten days more than hitherto at Blandings Castle and a few days at Wivelscombe Court, to which he had not so far been even invited.

It was after Kempton Park during Jeeves's second year at Worpley Maltravers, that Vaisey asked leave of absence to visit his ailing grandmother at Bury St. Edmunds. His devotion to her did him credit but his three weeks' absence might have seemed excessive had not Jeeves been able to take his place. When a similar period of absence followed his success at Doncaster it gradually dawned on the 3rd Earl that Vaisey's winnings were always spent on a prolonged orgy of dissipation. It also became apparent that his deputy, Jeeves, was a better valet than Vaisey had ever been. Vaisey's absence after Goodwood was thus made final, he being told that he need not return.

In this way it came about that Jeeves was replaced as second footman and promoted to the higher rank of valet. When the Earl attended the Cambridgeshire, Jeeves now accompanied him. When the Earl was at Newmarket, Jeeves too was there. He now deepened his knowledge of the turf, talking to stable hands, listening to trainers and even sometimes exchanging a greeting with a jockey in person, if not with an actual horse. To an encyclopaedic knowledge he now added snippets of inside information and mental pictures of the horses in training. For the rest of his life Jeeves was to be a persistent and successful backer of horses but one who never celebrated any success in champagne. Avoiding the mistake made by Vaisey and many another punter, he paid his winnings into a deposit account, building up the fortune on which he would eventually retire. It could never be said of Jeeves, however, that he refused to advise those who asked for his advice. He did not volunteer an opinion where none was asked but he willingly aided a friend. To illustrate this point one might quote from the *Memoirs* of Sir Roderick Carmoyle (p. 134). Sir Roderick asked Jeeves once whether he could spot the winner in tomorrow's Derby, and received the following reply:

'I fear not, Sir Roderick. It would seem to be an exceptionally open contest. Monsieur Boussac's Volent is, I understand, the favourite. Fifteen to two at last night's call over and the price likely to shorten to sixes or even fives for the S.P. But the animal in question is somewhat small and lightly boned for so gruelling an ordeal. Though we have, to be sure, seen such a handicap overcome. The case of Manna, the 1925 winner, springs to the mind, and Hyperion, another small horse, broke the course record previously held by Flying Fox, accomplishing the distance in two minutes, thirty-four seconds (*R.J.* p. 62).'

This was not an instance of Jeeves predicting the result but it serves to show the working of his powerful mind. Such being the intellectual level at which he moved, it is surprising that Lord Worplesdon never turned to him for advice. His Lordship would seem however, to have gone his own way, losing fairly consistently although on a small scale. When irritated beyond a certain point he would forswear betting and go off to the Argentine on business. In Jeeves's first year as his valet the 3rd Earl reached such a decision immediately after the Cesarewitch and decided to sail in the S.S. *Pink Pyjama* of 25 thousand tons, commanded by Captain Bastable. Jeeves, who had never been at sea before, was more than delighted at this prospect of seeing the world.

After watching Southampton recede astern, he paced the steerage deck and quickly made himself familiar with the parts of the ship, port and starboard, fore and aft. He could do little for his employer, he found, while the voyage lasted, for the stewards always beat him to it, but he could and did do something more to complete his education. He could think of himself thereafter as a man of the world who could begin an anecdote, 'One time in Rio . . .' or, 'Once when crossing the Atlantic . . .' He made friends with several of the crew and did his best to avoid ruining them when playing poker. Despite some rough weather, the voyage was a pleasant experience. The *Pink Pyjama* was a cargo ship, carrying only a dozen first-class passengers. None of those on board could claim any sort of equality with Lord Worplesdon, who spoke to only three of them. First of the favoured few, who made up a daily four at bridge, was Colonel Chuffnell, DSO, a cousin of Lord Chuffnell, well known at one time on the North West Frontier. Mrs Chuffnell, his wife, had been a Pendlebury-Davenport and so related, distantly, to the Duke of Dunstable. To make up the four was the Hon. Mr Digby Thistleton, the fifth and youngest son of the Duke and Duchess of Hampshire and normally resident with them in Cadogan Square (SW). The family estates had already been lost and the family, among ducal families, was the least prosperous. Mr Thistleton made his living by writing a gossip column and sought to make his fortune by marketing his inventions, no one of which had as yet proved successful. In sailing for the Argentine his professed object was to sell the current dictator* a device which would prevent all further disorder in the streets. Its exact nature was of course secret at the time but we now know that he had invented an anaesthetic spray which was guaranteed to reduce any rioting mob to somnolence in about thirty seconds. For this invention he was to ask the very reasonable price of a billion pesos but he did so without making a sale. On this outward journey he was optimistic, however, and in a cheerful mood. His was a typically Thistleton face, round and pink with a snub nose, all surmounted by curly dark hair, and he also had the well known family laugh, a braying noise which often caused alarm outside the haunts in which the sound was familiar. After an early period of rough weather the voyage was uneventful and the four bridge players settled down to their game in earnest, never quitting their table except for meals.

By a strange coincidence Lord Worplesdon and Mr Thistleton each carried a briefcase and both had been purchased from the same shop in Bond Street. They

---

* This was Sagrado Calamito, whose period in office was punctuated by risings, riots and attempted coups d'etat. He was finally driven from office and now lives quietly in Andalusia.

were identical in pattern and differed very little in colour but there the resemblance ended, for whereas his Lordship's case was full of company balance sheets, Mr Thistleton had filled his with samples of his inventive genius, including a sample bottle of his Mob Sedative (economy size). After an unusually convivial session one evening it was perhaps inevitable that there should be confusion over the briefcases, which were unwittingly swapped around. Nor do we learn with any surprise that Lord Worplesdon should have inadvertently knocked Mr Thistleton's case off his (Lord W's) dressing table, thus breaking the bottle of anaesthetic. The result, in theory, should have been to give his Lordship an unusually good night's sleep, but the formula used was still to be described as experimental. The stuff was more nearly lethal than its inventor intended and the 3rd Earl, when conscious again, was seriously ill and so remained for several days.

Having paid his lordship a perfunctory visit, saying, 'Hard cheese,' and, 'jolly bad luck', the other three bridge players went to the saloon and seated themselves dejectedly round their green baize battlefield.

'A grim situation,' said the Colonel.

'A bad show,' concluded Mr Thistleton and meant it, for he now had no sample to demonstrate.

'We *could* play three handed . . .?' said Mrs Chuffnell, but was told that this would not be the same. They discussed glumly the idea of recruiting one of the ship's officers but the Colonel would have none of it.

'They are always being called away to splice the whatnot or dance the hornpipe.' One or two other names were mentioned but the other passengers, if they played bridge at all, did so with appalling levity just as if card games were to be played for fun. The three spent a dull evening and next day told Lord Worplesdon that he was beng sorely missed.

He was still unfit to play but he made the suggestion that was to save them. 'Tell my man Jeeves to make a fourth – I'm told that he is a better player than I am.' Within the hour they were back at the table and the battle had begun. It finished shortly before they went ashore in Buenos Aires.

That Jeeves was an experienced card player was apparent as soon as he was called upon to shuffle. He did this with the rapid dexterity which one associates with motion pictures about old Southern gamblers on board Mississippi steamboats. That was only the prelude, however, to a play which was always sound and sometimes masterly. What clinched his reputation was the post-mortem he conducted on the afternoon of his first day at the table. Having cut for partners, Colonel Chuffnell had his wife for partner against Mr Thistleton and Jeeves. It was his call and he went one No Trump. Jeeves called Two Spades. Mrs Chuffnell, rather puzzled and knowing that she herself held four spades including the ace and Queen, bid 2 No Trumps. Mr Thistleton passed and the Colonel, thus encouraged, went on to 3 No Trumps, which Jeeves promply doubled. When the game was played Jeeves took seven tricks in Clubs, leaving his opponent down by three tricks.

'A good bluff!' admitted the Colonel. 'That was a game we should have won.'

'Was it my fault?' asked Mrs Chuffnell.

'Not at all, Ma'am,' said Jeeves. 'I held nothing except seven Clubs, including the four top honours, and a single useless Spade. My guess was that my opponents most probably had the Spades between them. If I called Clubs, the Colonel would probably have called another suit. So I made my bid, 2 Spades, to suggest that this was my strong suit. It was quite natural, Mrs Chuffnell, that you should bid 2 No Trumps for if I had the Spades your husband must be without them. So we played on the basis of his 3 No Trumps. Now, if I had called Clubs, you would have switched to a suit, probably Spades, and you would have won the game by five tricks.'

As from that day the others looked upon Jeeves with a new respect. He was at least as good a player as anyone else on board. As for Lord Worplesdon, he did not recover until after the voyage had ended.

The British influence which used to prevail in the Argentine left Buenos Aires with an impressive golf club and an equally impressive Racecourse,* one to which Lord Worplesdon was (naturally) attracted. So much was inevitable but the surprising thing is that he now showed a real talent for spotting the winner. Could it have been the result of his recent illness? Or was it due to the fact that the local sport was totally different and almost unbelievably crooked? The truth is, perhaps, that he had no claim here to local knowledge. Completely in the dark, he backed one horse because he liked its name, a second because of its jockey's colours, a third because he had met its owner at a cocktail party, and he thus gained better results than he had ever achieved by careful study.

He decided to prolong his visit and concluded at the same time that he must recruit a local valet who could read the sporting news in the original Spanish. He was also decidely miffed by a conversation in which Mr Thistleton had dwelt too heavily on Jeeves's ability as a bridge player. 'If you think so highly of this chap,' he had rejoined, 'you had best take him into your service.'

'Right – I'll do just that. It is awkward, I grant you, when a valet has more brains than his master.' The two men parted coldly and Jeeves soon found himself on the

---

* No man can be admitted to the enclosure who is not wearing a tie. There, or wherever such a rule exists, a tie may be hired from the barman for a fairly exorbitant fee. It is better than being left to play cards in the car park.

way back to England in a ship of the Green Funnel Line. Having failed to sell his Mob Sedative (having no sample of the stuff with which to demonstrate its usefulness) Mr Thistleton cut his visit short, having a new idea for a patent depilatory which he meant to place on the market in London. It was merely a watered down version of the Mob Sedative but he was convinced that it had a big potential. Nor as we shall see, were his hopes to be entirely disappointed.

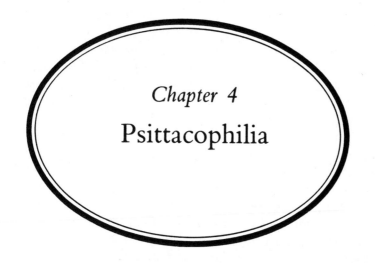

Chapter 4

Psittacophilia

Jeeves knew little about fashionable London until he came to live in Cadogan Square as valet to the Hon. Mr Digby Thistleton, well known for the gossip column he edited in the *Morning Courier*. Relatively impoverished as he may have been, Mr Thistleton's father, the Duke of Hampshire, still had his own valet, the elderly and reliable Mr Arthur Mitchell. It was he who proposed Jeeves as a member of the Junior Ganymede Club in Curzon Street and it was he who told Jeeves the salient facts about the Drones Club with premises at No. 16, Dover Street, Mayfair.

Always quick to learn, Jeeves soon realized that London is, for all practical purposes, an area bounded by Oxford Street on the North, by Regent Street on the East, by the Mall to the South and by Park Lane on the West. It was true, he discovered, that some people of consequence might live in a further area bounded by Knightsbridge, Grosvenor Place, Pimlico Road and Sloane Street. He had even been told that other people lived north of the Park in places like Lancaster Gate and Portman Square. Accepting such hearsay at its face value, he could still insist that life could not be lived to the full except in Mayfair. At its widest the world of fashion lies between Marble Arch, the Royal Mews, the Horse Guards Parade and St George's, Hanover Square. 'Whoever is tired of all that lies between those points is tired,' he would say, 'of life itself.'

The Junior Ganymede was a club with a membership restricted to gentlemen's personal gentlemen together with a few footmen and chauffeurs and a small and strictly limited number of butlers. The fact that it was the Junior Ganymede is enough to remind us that there was formerly an older club, the Ganymede proper, the membership of which was restricted to noblemen's personal noblemen. All that was long ago, however, and even the Junior Ganymede has gone the way of other noble institutions. In its great days the Junior G. was perhaps chiefly famous for its Club Book, compiled under Rule 11, to which members contributed the fullest information about their employers, including an estimate of their intelligence (if any) on a Scale marked from 1 to 10 and a final assessment of their relative sanity. To these basic facts were added some notes about hobbies and habits, lapses and loves, with anecdotes added to illustrate character or generally to entertain the members of the Club. It was while studying this Club Book that Jeeves came to realize that the Junior Ganymede's bachelor employers were nearly all of them members of the Drones Club, the existence of which had been revealed to him by Arthur Mitchell. What he failed at first to understand was what exactly the Drones had in common with each other. After patient inquiry he was able, however, to satisfy himself that their qualifications for entry were purely negative. At other Clubs, he discovered, the members all served (or had served) in the Brigade or the Cavalry, were active in the Tory or Liberal interest, were prominent in the Church or on the stage, had attended one or other of the two universities, or had at least been pupils at a leading public school. The Drones were young men who had escaped every category except possibly the last. No one of them could be said to have achieved anything, not even so much as a commission or a degree. Each of them possessed, however, an income or an allowance and all of them circulated, when in town, within the tribal boundaries which we have been at pains to define. Their clothes were correct, their ties matched their socks and they nearly all employed as valet a member of the Junior Ganymede.

Typical Drones member was the Hon. Mr Digby Thistleton himself. Once you have admitted that he was the youngest son of a fairly progenitive and impecunious Duke you have said it all. He was privately educated and could seemingly play a tolerable hand at bridge. We have no reason to suppose that he could ride, shoot, fish or swim. If he could play the guitar there is no recorded instance of his having done so. All that singles him out from the other Drones is that he possessed ambition and a measure of enterprise. Who but he would have tried to market a mob-dispersal mist in Buenos Aires? A cellar in Curzon Street was his laboratory and he worked there for hours. It seemed, however, to Jeeves that he spent more time, relatively, on plans for marketing and publicity. 'It is not *what* you sell that matters,' he would explain, 'but *how* you sell it.' His friends would agree absently, tapping their heads and exchanging significant glances as soon as they were out of sight.

Time was to prove, however, that he was right and that they were wrong. This was far from apparent, though, when he first tried to place Antibarb on the market. This was a depilatory (sired by Mob Sedative out of Tapwater) which had the most painful effect on the skin. By way of testing the market it was first offered for sale in a restricted area south of the river. Far from being a success, it brought Mr Thistleton (Tubby to his friends) a spate of vituperative correspondence from Bermondsey. Reading between the lines and ignoring the misspelling of the more abstruse words like blackguard, the Managing Director of the Mayfair Pharmaceutical Company – that is, Tubby – was given to understand that his product did not serve the purpose for which it was sold. Hair, it seemed, was practically the only thing which it did not destroy. He was told, indeed, of instances in which it had paralysed a retired policeman and killed at least one pet rabbit in a litter of three. Tubby was puzzled over this and simply refused to believe that his mixture could serve no useful purpose. His motto 'There is always a way' was repeated daily with growing emphasis but diminishing confidence. Its truth was proved, however, on the morning when the fan mail comprised only a single letter postmarked from Jamaica Road. The sender, in demanding her money back, stated that Antibarb had actually encouraged the growth of the underarm hair which she had been trying to remove. Discouraged at first, Tubby then had his flash of inspiration. What he had discovered was a hair restorer and should now be marketed as such.

After prolonged thought he decided to call it Hair – O, using as his first advertisement his picture of a billiard ball before and after the stuff had been applied. Was it effective? Any generalization on this point would be rash but we know of at least one case in which the remedy failed to produce any visible result. Jeeves had by this time in his career a receding hairline which would have added to his dignity as a butler but which detracted a little from what had so far been a youthful appearance. After four months of regular application the tide had ebbed by another centimetre. Gazing into the mirror, Jeeves had to admit to himself that the onset of middle age had fairly begun.

If Jeeves had this inner feeling of sadness, his employer, Digby Thistleton, was on top of the world. The Mayfair Pharmaceutical Company had moved to larger premises, no longer in a basement, Mr Thistleton had quit the parental home and moved to a penthouse flat in Park Lane. He was already a respected member of the Carlton Club, having resigned from the Drones, where he was known now to be richer than Oofy Prosser, and there were rumours already about his impending knighthood. This never transpired because his contributions to the party fund were too generous. He was presently given a peerage instead and entered the House of Lords as the Rt. Hon. Lord Bridgeworth. By that time Jeeves had ceased to be his valet and for a reason which need cause us no surprise. It was plainly impossible for the Chairman of the Mayfair Pharmaceutical Group to employ a servant with a receding hairline. He had no complaint at all about Jeeves's character or work. His only failure, as Jeeves readily understood, was as a living advertisement for Hair – O. A replacement had to be found and Lord Bridgeworth bade Jeeves a reluctant farewell.

'I have written you a testimonial,' he concluded, 'in the strongest terms. More than that, however, I have found you what should prove a good situation with a friend of mine, Lord Brancaster. You may perhaps have heard of him?'

'No, my Lord.'

'That is understandable. Lord Brancaster is not much in the public eye except when appearing at school speech days. He is also, however, a well known psittacophile, a fact of which you should not lose sight.'

'Yes, my Lord. It is good of your Lordship to bear my

interests in mind. I shall endeavour to justify your kind recommendation.'

In the years to come, with more worldly experience, Jeeves would have understood the word psittacophile. It will be a term familiar to many readers of this book although few perhaps will have much occasion to make use of it. But Jeeves, like many of us, was reluctant to admit his ignorance of a word he might hear for the first time. Hearing that Lord Brancaster was a psittacophile his immediate instinct was to say 'How very sad. Is it supposed that his Lordship will die of the complaint?' His next idea might have been to remark that Britain must have many immigrants from Psittacophilia, all of them said to be prosperous. He could again have said that he was free from religious prejudices and only too glad that the psittacophiles should worship in their own way. On the other hand it might transpire that Psittacophile might be his lordship's surname, the family having been prominent in Asia Minor for centuries past.

Faced with all these possibilities, Jeeves wisely made no comment at all. He went instead to the Junior Ganymede and discovered at once that Lord Brancaster was not and had never been represented there by any present or previous valet. It was almost as easy to ascertain that he was not, nor had ever been, a member of the Drones. He did, however, appear in *Debrett* and from his entry in that work it was clear that his name, apart from his title, was Nigel Strickland Davenant Rokely Fox-Medlicott. It was as manifest that he was the eldest son of the 4th Baron and that he had so far no other claim to fame. If there was anything abnormal about his description it was that his family seat, Rokely Towers,* was in

---

* Rokely Towers was in its day a Gothic Castle of some note requiring an army of servants to maintain the Fox-Medlicotts in a state of considerable discomfort. It was burnt down in 1933, all but the east wing, and a lawsuit followed in which the Buzzard Insurance Company maintained that Hil-

Cheshire whereas he actually lived, seemingly, at a far less impressive address in Surrey; the Elms, Titteridge, near Hazelmere. His entry in *Who's Who* was very brief but it appeared from this that he was governor of a number of schools but of none which would often feature in the more glossy periodicals. A certain famous scholastic agency has been said to use the following classification: Category I *Leading Public Schools*; Category II *Well-known Public Schools*; Category III *Good Schools*; and, finally, Category IV *Schools*. The institutions with which Lord Brancaster was connected could nearly all be placed without hesitation in Category IV. He belonged to no London Club but was Vice President of the Psittacophilic Association or rather of its British Branch. He was unmarried and, not unreasonably, childless. His family motto was 'Speak thy Mind' and his heir would be a cousin now employed (like thousands of other people) by the Race Relations Board.

Beyond the facts listed in *Debrett*, Jeeves drew blank. He approached Hazelmere, therefore, when the day came, with a completely open mind. He could say, with the Duke of Orleans when speaking of the Dauphin in *Henry V* (Act III, Scene 7) 'He never did harm, that I heard of,' but could feel, as did the Constable of France, that such tepid praise warns us not to expect too much. The Elms turned out to be what it sounds like, a comfortable, redbrick villa standing amidst fir trees and facing a semi-circular drive. As he trod the gravel and looked about him, hearing his taxi drive away, Jeeves appeared as a more than respectable figure in his dark suit and bowler hat, carrying his suitcase in one hand, his umbrella in the other. He admired in passing a sunlit

---

debrand, the 3rd Baron, had deliberately set the place alight. Proof was insufficient and the Company had eventually to pay up. The estate is still in the family, the east wing being in use as a country cottage.

statue of Garibaldi, perhaps, or John the Baptist, and looked with interest at the fretwork which added such character to the dormer windows. After tugging at the bell-pull, he was presently admitted by a housemaid called Elsie, who showed him into the study and told him to wait there while she apprised Lord Brancaster of his arrival. Some minutes passed and Jeeves found himself increasingly puzzled by the sounds he heard from the back of the house. The noise was muffled by the solidity of the Victorian brickwork but it sounded like a committee meeting at which everyone was talking at once. There was outspoken disagreement between the members present and many of them repeated themselves with emphasis but not quite distinctly enough for him to hear the actual words said.

Foiled over this, Jeeves looked around him and saw that most of the books on the shelves had to do with Ornithology. On the walls, he noticed, were engravings or photographs of schools like Brancaster High School, Dymchurch College and Market Snodsbury Grammar School. Could Lord Brancaster have attended all these schools or indeed any of them? Jeeves toyed with the idea of his Lordship having been successively expelled from one institution after another but then he noticed that several of these schools were for girls. Baffled again, Jeeves reflected that education is a field in which too much is worse than none. To have been at Eton and Harrow, Oxford and Cambridge, is to arouse not respect but suspicion. At this point Jeeves suddenly remembered that Lord Brancaster was addicted to school governorship. These were evidently the schools to which he stood, as it were, as patron. At all of them his function was merely to give away the prizes, so warmly consoling the non-recipients as to make the prize winners actually ashamed of themselves. A picture of the new Science Block at Worrell could thus be said to explain itself. His lordship had cut the tape and declared it open. He might, by contrast, have laid the foundation stone, but the principle is much the same. What remained a mystery was his evident addiction to this sort of thing. Here was a man, it would seem, who must scan the obituaries to learn what vacancies were arising on what board of governors. Having seen his opportunity, he must then write to his friends, use his political influence, call on the headmaster and send bottles of port (where appropriate) to the Dean and Chapter. He was to be pictured as waiting tensely to hear whether his candidature had succeeded. If this were actually Lord Brancaster's way of life, Jeeves concluded, the man must be completely off his head.

Before his thoughts went any further, Jeeves heard the door open and, rising, he saw Lord Brancaster in person. His lordship was a small but colourful figure, wearing a green velvet jacket, a yellow pullover, purple shirt, light blue tie and red socks. He actually wore trousers as well but these, being grey, attracted less attention. His fair hair was plastered flat and sleek with brilliantine, his sallow face was expressionless and his hooked nose had an almost sinister curve. He looked sharply to left and right, as if fearing an ambush, and then fixed Jeeves with an unwinking eye.

'I am Jeeves, my lord, and I have brought your lordship a letter from Lord Bridgeworth, formerly Mr Digby Thistleton.'

'I see, I see, I see,' said Lord Brancaster as he opened the letter. His voice was high and shrill, his last word being uttered with something like a shriek. Having read the letter, he tore it to pieces and let the fragments fall to the carpet.

'I shall endeavour to give satisfaction, my lord,' said Jeeves helpfully.

'You will, you will, you will? No doubt, no doubt, no

doubt. Yes, yes, yes. Now come with me, come with me.' Jeeves followed his lordship down a corridor which led to the back of the house. The background noise grew louder and reached a crescendo as the back door was thrown open. Following his new employer, Jeeves stepped into a large aviary, each section of which was filled with parrots of a different size and hue. There was a central passageway and Lord Brancaster passed slowly along it, his head jerking from side to side, his mouth opening and shutting with a snap. The noise was deafening, however, and Jeeves could hear nothing at all of what was being said. One problem at least was solved. A psittacophile is one who dotes on a parrot or parrots and there could be no doubt about Lord Brancaster's claim to be Vice-President (at least) of any association to which the world's psittacophiles might belong.

Jeeves's senses reeled as he ran the gauntlet between parrots calling, 'Pretty boy, pretty boy', and others shrieking, 'Hallo, dear, hallo dear, drinks on the house, on the house, on the house.' They passed through a door in a brick wall and the noise diminished abruptly:

'. . . there are over five hundred species, you see, and this aviary is divided regionally as between South America, Indonesia, Australia and the Pacific. We have now reached the cages set aside for the parrots from Asia and Africa.'

'Are there fewer of those, my lord?'

'Fewer of those, fewer of those. Yes, they are fewer, fewer. It is the grey ones, the grey ones of Africa who do most of the talk talking.'

'They don't actually seem as noisy, my lord.'

'They aren't as noisy, but they make sense when they speak they speak. I call this cage Pygmalian corner. That one, the male, I call Higgins. That one, the female, I call Eliza. Now, listen, listen, listen. Come on, Higgins, say your piece, say your piece.' Higgins shuffled along his perch and then shuffled back again, evidently trying to decide on a policy.

After a pregnant pause he suddenly squawked, 'The rains in Spain fall mainly in the plain.'

An instant later Eliza replied, 'The rines in Spine fall minely in the pline,' and then said it twice more, to be on the safe side. Higgins was quick to correct her, after which he lapsed into silence.

His lordship strolled on, drawing attention to this bird and that. He finally stopped outside a large cage containing but a single grey parrot. He was evidently a favourite for his cage was furnished with every hoop and swing a parrot could possibly want and some of which no other parrot could even have heard.

'This is Lars Porsena, Porsena.'

'Indeed, my lord?'

'You will remember Macaulay's poem?'

'Yes, my lord, "By the nine gods he swore."'

'Just so, just so, just so. Well, Jeeves, it will be your task to fetch Lars Porsena each morning at seven-thirty precisely and bring him to my bedroom. After that, bring me my morning morning tea with two digestive biscuits, one for each of us each of us.'

'Very good, very good, very good, my lord,' replied Jeeves. 'How am I to carry him, carry him?'

'He will sit on your shoulder. Don't worry, Jeeves, he is quite harmless as a rule.' Lord Brancaster glanced involuntarily at a piece of sticking-plaster on his left fore finger. 'You'll be good friends in no time at all, no time at all at all at all.'

Jeeves found himself remembering a line from the works of Mark Twain: 'She was not quite what you would call refined. She was not quite what you would call unrefined. She was the kind of person that keeps a parrot.' More precisely, as Jeeves now realized, she had been a psittacophile.

Jeeves was shown his attic room and later came down for the midday meal in the kitchen. There were four other servants with the cook, Mrs Buttley, in the chair. She bade Jeeves welcome against a background noise which was still all too audible.

'You will have noticed, Mr Jeeves, that Lord Brancaster is fond of parrots, of parrots?'

'Yes, yes. Fond of parrots he must be, must be.'

'It's quieter after sunset,' said Elsie kindly. 'They sleep when it's dark, it's dark.'

'When it's dark, that's good. But why is his lordship so keen on education. Why all those pictures of schools in his study? He believes, maybe, in learning parrot fashion?'

'It's not that, not that,' replied Elsie, 'I once heard one of his lordship's aunts talking about it when he wasn't there wasn't there. She said it was by way of compensation sort of.'

'I don't quite see . . .'

'Well, some days he can't hear himself think because of the noise from his parrots all talking at once. So his idea of a change and a rest is to go somewhere different, where he can do the talking and his audience has to listen. That means a school speech day with him as chairman of the governors. He comes back feeling ever so much better.'

'Ever so much better . . . His pleasure is in having a captive audience . . .'

'A captive audience, and they won't get their prizes until he's said all he wants to say.'

'Wants to say . . . Mrs Buttley, we are all talking like parrots!'

'Of course, Mr Jeeves, how can we help it?' There was a long silence in which Jeeves decided to join.

Next morning, Jeeves went to fetch Lars Porsena and was relieved to find that the bird perched on his shoulder without reluctance. His walk back to the house was without incident until he reached the back door, at which point his feathered passenger suddenly squawked, 'Damn you, sir' and 'Bloody Hell.' Mounting the stairs with patience and care he was abruptly told to 'Watch it, you ****** *****!' All went well, however, until he reached Lord Brancaster's bedroom door, at which point the parrot, unprovoked, bit his left ear. As he entered the room he was trying to staunch the blood with a handkerchief.

'Ah, sorry about that, Jeeves,' said Lord Brancaster. 'You'll find sticking-plaster on the dressing-table. I always always keep it handy.'

Depositing Lars Porsena on the rail at the foot of the bed, Jeeves withdrew to the bathroom, bleeding profusely. When it comes to bleeding, the ear, as compared with other parts of the anatomy, is in a class by itself. Jeeves made this discovery for himself but eventually succeeded in his effort at damage control. Once sufficiently patched up, he brought Lord Brancaster his tea and a couple of digestive biscuits. He then ran the bath and presently reported to his lordship that his bath was ready.

'Thank you, Jeeves. You can now take Lars Porsena back to his cage.'

'Very good, my lord,' said Jeeves and hurried from the room. When he returned, a few minutes later, he was carrying the plastic lid of the dustbin. Allowing the parrot to perch on his shoulder again, he now placed the plastic shield between his head and the creature's beak. Thus protected, he descended the stairs once more, listening to a stream of bad language which would have done credit to any criminal, punctuated by the rap of beak on plastic.

That evening Lord Brancaster asked Jeeves to fetch Lars Porsena again, this time for what he described as a regular after dinner chat. Jeeves might have repeated his trick with the dustbin lid but he could not bring himself to bring such an article into the dining-room. He decided, therefore, on a more scientific approach. He soaked a biscuit in non-vintage port and gave it to the parrot in its cage. It accepted the gift without suspicion but held it with difficulty when the journey began. Once it had reached Lord Brancaster's presence, it seemed, for a while that Lars Porsena intended to sing. He gave up that idea, however, and was placed in a cage at his lordship's elbow, where he swore quietly to himself for a while, then suddenly capsized, lying on the floor of the cage, with his feet in the air. He had passed out, losing all further interest in the proceedings.

At much the same time Jeeves came to a decision which he kept for the time to himself. Waiting until all was quiet, he went to his room and packed. Without making a sound, he let himself out of the front door, suitcase in hand, and made his way towards the station. It was late, it was dark and he had booked no room for the night. His case was heavy and it might rain at any moment. He had no home, no family, no friends to whom he could turn. For all that, his decision had been made. He would not stay at the Elms for another night, not even for another hour.

It is important, however, that we should understand his motive. He did not quit because his ear had been bitten. He did not leave because of the hideous noise. As Petruchio said, 'Think you a little din can haunt mine ears?' With the noise alone he could have coped. What he had found intolerable was the way Lord Brancaster dressed. He could not act as a valet for someone whose clothes were not those of a gentleman. Finding himself in an impossible position, he had no alternative but to go and stand not upon the order of his going. As he trudged through the darkness he asked himself:

Whether 'tis nobler in the mind to suffer
The stings and parrots of outrageous fortune,
Or to take arms against a sea of troubles
And by opposing end them?

He had hesitated, to be sure, before taking the decisive step, wondering whether he might not regret this leap into the unknown. Should he not find another place before resigning the one he had? Is not this the thought which makes us pause:

And makes us rather bear those ills we have
Than fly to others that we know not of?
Thus conscience does make cowards of us all;
And thus the native hue of resolution
Is sicklied o'er with the pale cast of thought;
And enterprises of great pith and moment,
With this regard, their currents turn awry,
And lose the name of action . . .

(Hamlet, Act III Scene I)

But Jeeves persisted in his resolve and his enterprise retained the name of action. More than that, he was lucky, being offered a lift by a passing motorist, who left him at the station itself; just in time, as it chanced, for the last train to London.

At the Junior Ganymede next day, having slept at a small hotel near Charing Cross, Jeeves met up with his old friend, Arthur Mitchell.

'So you have quit the service of Lord Brancaster,' said Arthur. 'You never told me that you were to work for him. I could have warned you, lad, and I warn you now in words you should remember: *Beware of Dumbchummery* Steer clear of it! Avoid it like the plague!'

'*DUMB* – chummery?' Jeeves exclaimed.

'Well, not dumb in this case but the principle is the

same. People who are crazy about animals make life hell for their servants. Stick to bachelors, by all means, and have nothing to do with people who are poor, but look out for talk about horses and dogs, cats and canaries. When you hear it, turn back in time and look elsewhere!'

'You are right, Arthur, but I have learnt my lesson. Have you heard, by chance, of a vacancy which might suit me?'

'Well, it so happens that I have. I've been told that Lord Frederick Ranelagh has recently lost his valet – a fellow called Sam Bennings, until recently a member of this club.'

'But how did Lord Frederick come to lose him?'

'Sam won a large sum on the football pools. He is setting up a dry-cleaning business in Brighton.'

'In Brighton?'

'I should perhaps have said in Hove. Anyway, Lord Frederick has been looking for a possible successor. It is my impression that you could do worse. He keeps no parrots so far as I know.'

'Arthur,' said Jeeves, 'you are a real friend. More than most of us you deserve the proud name of a gentleman's personal gentleman. The drinks are on me! Barman! The same again, please. And now forgive me if I desert you for a few minutes. I have urgent business which cannot wait.'

'I quite understand and I often feel the same, more often now indeed than when I was a younger man.'

'I don't mean that, Arthur. My urgent business is with the Club Book. I must look up the entry under "Ranelagh, Lord Frederick". One can't be too careful. After all, he might keep alligators!'

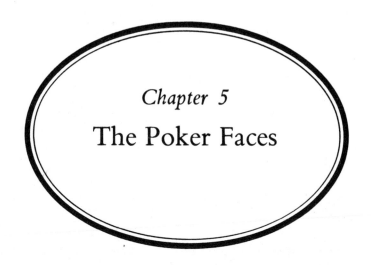

Chapter 5

The Poker Faces

The Junior Ganymede Club Book is so planned that each entry includes the answers to certain definite questions, after which there are blank pages for general comment and anecdote: the result reading as follows in this particular case:–

NAME/TITLE: Frederick Augustus Lonsdale Hedley, otherwise known as Lord Frederick Ranelagh.
FAMILY: He is second son of the Old Marquis of Southwark and therefore the younger brother of the present Marquis, who owns extensive property in the Borough.* The Marquis married one of C. B. Cochran's Young Ladies and has five children by her, three of them male.
BORN: Date unknown.

---

* The Hedley family own a considerable part of the Borough and derives from this estate the bulk of the family's income. The present Marquis, Lord Frederick's elder brother, was once accused in the press of owning all the brothels in Southwark but he had no difficulty in showing that they all belonged to the Ecclesiastical Commissioners.

STATUS: Bachelor.

EDUCATED: Harrow.

INCOME: Insufficient. Lord F. has a small income of his own and will have more if and when his mother dies. She lives and will probably live for ever at her villa near Cannes, where she often expresses her regret that Lord F. has never married an heiress. He has, in addition, an allowance from the family estate but this is plainly inadequate.

INTELLIGENCE: Grade 7 (Maximum 10)

ADDRESS: c/o Barclay's Bank, Monte Carlo.

OTHER SERVANTS: French chef, two Italian stewards, one boy.

PETS: None.

HOBBIES: Entertaining American guests, yachting and tennis.

VIRTUES: Sobriety.

FAILINGS: He is mean.

GENERAL: Lord F. has rooms in Albany but lives for most of the year on board his schooner *Vortex II*, at permanent moorings in the harbour at Monte Carlo. Since her engines and sails were removed, the yacht has been a fixture, luxuriously fitted and furnished, impressive in appearance and often the largest yacht in the harbour. Lord F.'s partner is Colonel Alistair McVane. His role is to make friends ashore with wealthy American visitors. If they have wives he offers (for a consideration) to arrange for them to dine on board *Vortex II* as guests of Lord F. If they have daughters the invitation is accompanied by a hint that Lord F. is an eligible bachelor, some day to be a Marquis (but see above under *family*). If the men are travelling alone he invites them on board for a game of poker. In either event Lord F. and Colonel M. split the proceeds fifty-fifty. It is a question whether Lord F. would really marry an heiress. It would solve his main problem but he is not interested in girls, having (it is believed) a mother fixation. Girls sense this and lose interest in about a week. He once entertained an attractive blonde who turned out to be a manicurist at the Monte Carlo Hilton. Another time he was confronted by a Texan who could really play poker. On both occasions he was suddenly taken ill. I was with Lord F. for two years and left him when offered the more lucrative post of butler with Mr Hank Hochstrasse of Akron, Ohio.

RECOMMENDATION: OK if you like Monte Carlo.

SIGNED: William Hockley.

Jeeves had never been to the South of France and saw this as a good opportunity to travel. Having finished his drink and thanked Arthur Mitchell for his advice, he went round at once to Albany and applied for the vacancy. Lord Frederick turned out to be slim and handsome, well dressed, athletic and sunburnt, with all outward symptoms of eligible bachelorhood. He wore a monocle and had cultivated an air of feckless stupidity which might well disarm the American mother of an available daughter.

'So you were with Digby Thistleton, what?'

'Yes, Lord Frederick. Now Lord Bridgeworth.'

'Did you resign or were you fired?'

'I was fired, Lord Frederick. He could not retain a valet with a receding hair line.'

'It wouldn't do, what! But how did he come to employ you in the first place. Eh?'

'The ointment now sold as a hair restorer was then on the market as a depilatory.'

'A useful all purpose discovery, what, what?'

'It has proved highly remunerative.'

'And Lord B. had nothing else against you?'

'I suggest, with due deference, Lord Frederick, that you ask him yourself. I have written his telephone number on this sheet of notepaper.'

'Very well then, I'll do just that.'

After a short conversation Lord Frederick, still holding the receiver, turned to Jeeves again.

'Lord Bridgeworth is astonished. He thought that you had accepted employment with Lord Brancaster.'

'I did, Lord Frederick. He has too many parrots and one of them bit me.' He pointed to the sticking-plaster on his left ear.

Lord Frederick spoke again into the receiver: 'Jeeves says that Brancaster has too many parrots. Ah, I see. You say he was warned about that? Lord B. is a *what*, did you say? Perhaps you had better spell it, eh?'

Jeeves managed to intervene at this point.

'I was warned, Lord Frederick, that Lord Brancaster is a psittacophile but did not at that time know what the word meant.'

'What the deuce does it mean, eh?'

'One who is crazy about parrots.'

Lord Frederick turned back to the telephone: 'All right. I've got the message now. I think that Jeeves was right to desert Brancaster. What else could he do, what? Was he a good valet while with you? He was, eh? . . . A useful chap, what? . . . Well, thanks very much. Goodbye.'

Lord Frederick rang off and said to Jeeves, 'He speaks well of you. What more have you to say for yourself?'

'Well, it occurs to me, Lord Frederick, that you might want a man who is willing to play a different part on occasion, as deckhand, as coxswain of a boat, as mate or boatswain of *Vortex II.*'

'So you have heard of my schooner and you think that your seamanship is good enough?'

'Good enough, Lord Frederick, for *Vortex II.*'

'Very well then. You may consider yourself a member of the crew. Report to me here on Thursday at 10 am and have your baggage and passport ready. We leave on that day by the Blue Train. If you don't yet speak French, now is the time to learn, what?'

It would be true to say that Jeeves completed his education at Monte Carlo. It was there he learnt how to play different parts, now as a travelling valet, now as a bluff seadog and then again as a bodyguard or private detective. He never became exactly fluent in French but he learnt enough for every normal purpose. He came to realize that a casino is a place to avoid. It would be an exaggeration to say that he became familiar with the underworld but he soon grasped the fact that Lord Frederick was, as compared with some other people, a relatively honest man. It could not be said of Lord F. that he really meant much harm. More than that, he could claim as did Verges, that he was, 'as honest as any man living that is an old man and no honester than I'. Jeeves was left with few illusions. While willing to assist in his employer's manoeuvres, and 'sordid' is the word which best describes them, there was a point, Jeeves decided, beyond which he would not go. Faced by actual crime, he was on the side of the police; and the police, round Monte Carlo, had plenty, but plenty, to keep them occupied. It was on board *Vortex II* that he learnt how to control his expression and remain completely impassive. It was important for Lord Frederick to present himself as a man of almost boundless wealth. His yacht must seem to have a crew of about twelve, quite apart from the skipper and chef. His launch would be manned by coxswain and ship's boy. Once the ship had been reached, the first officer would appear and the visitors would later see, besides the two cabin stewards, the boatswain, the deck steward and the barman. A series of minimal and quickly assumed disguises could serve the purpose because the guests, after all, would take no particular notice of the crew, gaining merely a vague impression of numbers and efficiency.

Autobiographies written at this time by film stars and nonentities alike often make passing mention of *Vortex II*: 'Conspicuous in the harbour was the beautiful schooner owned by Lord Frederick Ranelagh. Dining on board her one evening, I found that my fellow guests were etc. etc.'* Residents in Monte Carlo were later to smile at passages like this. Some of them knew that invitations to this particular yacht were not really hard to come by – but had, of course, to be paid for.

Remembering this period of his life, Jeeves was to say afterwards that Colonel McVane was not quite as clever a man as he supposed himself to be. He admittedly looked the part, having a fine figure, military bearing and a suitably clipped grey moustache. His intelligence system rested upon head porters of the more expensive hotels who alerted him when any promising guests arrived. As from that point his method of making casual contact was masterly, as a rule, and merely adjusted to each situation. Where he went astray on occasion, was in failing to realize that some people are less vulnerable – and even more dangerous – than they seem. This is how disaster loomed on one occasion after Jeeves had been in Monte Carlo for about three months.

On the day in question McVane had word of an American family just arrived at the Hotel Metropole. It comprised, as McVane heard from a usually reliable source, a Mr and Mrs Schuyler Schwartz, Jun., of Houston, Texas, with a daughter called Griselda (aged about 27) and a son called Wilbur (aged about 19). There was good reason to believe that Mr Schwartz was extremely wealthy, and Mrs Schwartz was socially ambitious, that

* *No life misspent*, Douglas Dundreary, London, 1951.

the daughter (who was anything but pretty) must be desperate for a husband and that the son must be bored to tears. Detailed information about McVane's technique is not easy to obtain but Jeeves came to know that it hinged upon a bogus connection with the Palace. Having aroused the victim's interest with talk about the wealthy bachelor, heir to the Marquis of Southwark, he would confess that invitations were hard to come by. Lord Frederick was very careful about making casual acquaintances, some of whom might try to take advantage of him. But dinner aboard Lord Frederick's yacht was quite an experience. She was built in 1909 and the saloon was an Edwardian work of art in polished mahogany – something really out of this world – that and the Georgian silver with the dishes produced by Jean Pierre . . . After some thought the Colonel would have a sudden inspiration. If Lord Frederick were to receive an appeal from the Palace he could not well refuse. The story would be that the Prince had invited some American friends of his to dine while forgetting that he was himself to be a guest that evening of the Archbishop. Would Lord Frederick be good enough to entertain his dear friends that evening – he would himself invite them another day? Astonished, the victim would ask whether the Prince could be persuaded to do this? No, would be the answer: the Prince would know nothing about it. Lord Frederick would receive the request from the Prince's ADC with the connivance of the Major Domo and other court officials. The Colonel had a friend in the Palace, it so happened. There was no certainty that this plan would succeed – the Colonel thought that it was, at best, an outside chance. If it succeeded, however, a few people would expect to be bribed . . . It was shocking, really, but that was the local custom. The Colonel would keep the expense to a minimum but . . . He would end by naming a sum.

Watching the sequence of events, Jeeves remembered on Ode written by the poet Gray:

> *Alas, regardless of their doom*
>   *the little victims play:*
> *No sense have they of ills to come*
>   *Nor care beyond to-day . . .*

In fact it may be doubed whether many Americans really believed what McVane told them, but, true or not, the story would form the basis for a good anecdote to tell back in Minneapolis or Buffalo. 'The Prince sent his apologies but we dined instead with Lord Frederick Ranelagh. The harbour was moonlit and his yacht . . .', etc. The wife would fall for this, anyway, and much the more so if she had an unmarried daughter. On most of these occasions the Colonel would invite another couple to make the thing less contrived and his chosen guests on this evening were the American couple, Mr and Mrs Standish G. Lowell, whose cabin cruiser was moored at no great distance from *Vortex II*. From the Schwartz point of view the Lowells would make quite a pretty addition to any subsequent name-dropping.

When the party assembled, the scene fell in no way short of the preliminary advertising. The moon was reflected in the still waters of the harbour. The schooner was a vision of white and gold. The candles and silverware, the orchids and crystal were all reflected in the dark polished mahogany. The host was glamorous and affable, the dinner jackets were tropical, the frocks were revealing, the service was impeccable, the dinner was memorable, the wines were vintage and the decanters circulated just as they should. Nor can it be said that it was really a swindle. It was as aristocratic a party as money could buy and the Colonel would have said that it was cheap at the price. Lord Frederick sat at the head of the table with Mrs Lowell on his right, Mrs Schwartz on his left. The Colonel sat at the foot of the table with Miss Schwartz on his left, Mr Schwartz on his right. Mr Lowell sat next to Mrs Schwartz and young Mr Schwartz next to Mrs Lowell. Acting now as chief steward, Jeeves hovered over the table in white uniform, controlling his two assistants with soundless gestures. He would have said, at this stage, that all was well. Mr Schuyler Schwartz was clearly, it is true, a tough character and no fool. He had gone along with the charade to please his wife, for whom this was seemingly the event of her lifetime. Their daughter was a plain woman of powerful build and spotty complexion, whose eyes were fixed hungrily on Lord Frederick. Their son, Wilbur, was a feeble creature by comparison with a large head, pale face, and thick lensed spectacles. He said little but looked about him with the air of one assessing the value of the yacht and contents. It was clearly only a question of time before he asked some question about the engines. The Lowells were full of information about their own cruiser, the *Nantucket* which must have been a new toy. She had, apparently, every safety device in the world, which was more that could be said about *Vortex II*; the safety of which was secured, of course, on a different principle.

After dinner, or anyway after coffee, the party split up. Mrs Lowell took Mrs Schwartz over to see the *Nantucket*. Miss Griselda begged Lord Frederick to show her the chart of the harbour and coastline. Colonel McVane asked the other guests, Mr Schwartz, Mr Lowell and Mr Wilbur Schwartz, whether they would care for a game of Draw Poker. When they accepted this invitation, the card table being set up in the after saloon, Jeeves withdrew to the galley, where he had his own meal with the chef. After that and a glass of wine he went on deck in order to see what was happening.

Each saloon had a skylight, through which any observant person – and Jeeves was nothing if not observant – could follow events without much difficulty. And what he saw on this occasion was profoundly disturbing. In the chartroom below the wheelhouse Lord Frederick had been driven into a corner and was probably on the point of surrender. Griselda's frock had come apart, revealing much to admire but little in the way of underwear. The situation was evidently grave, if not critical (which is the worse? – a moot point.) In the after saloon, on the other hand, the situation was a great deal more adverse. To judge by the position of the chips and the expression on the Colonel's face, the poker game was a mere massacre, played for high stakes, with the brainy and expressionless Wilbur repeatedly taking the pool. The point had been reached when someone had to do something to save the situation. In a roughly similar crisis, described by Shakespeare in *The Tempest*, the mariners cried, 'All lost! to prayers, to prayers! all lost!' It is a question however, whether these lamentations can have been a real help. Making a quick decision, Jeeves dashed to his cabin, changed into his off-duty clothes, added a cloth cap and, pulling it well down over his eyes, used a scarf to hide the lower half of his face. Grabbing Lord Frederick's shotgun, he threw open the door of the after-saloon, shouting, 'Hands up, everybody!' The poker players raised their hands and he made them stand back against the bulkhead. 'Now all of you put your wallets on the table. Go on – all you have! I'll shoot the man who holds anything back.' After sweeping the chips and cards off the table and collecting the cash, he drove the four poker players into the pantry and locked them in.

A minute later he shouted, 'Hands up!' to Lord Frederick and Griselda, breaking up the clinch in the nick of time. He drove Lord Frederick into the boatswain's store and Griselda into the empty sailroom, locking both doors after them. Five minutes later he changed back into chief steward's uniform, fired both barrels of the gun, made noises of conflict, being joined in this by the other two stewards, and finally releasing the captives, telling them that he had retaken the ship and that the unknown gunman had fled in his own boat.

Acting on Jeeves's advice, Colonel McVane now took the launch, with the ship's boy, and went off to fetch the police. The two ladies returned from the cabin cruiser and were relieved to learn that no one had been hurt. Lord Frederick pressed brandy on everyone and apologized deeply that such a disaster should fall on his guests. Griselda burst into floods of tears, a natural reaction after the danger was past. Her mother assured her that all was well but that she had better put on her overcoat. Mr Schwartz looked grim and said 'I'll be darned! If only I'd had my gun!' All the victims showed sympathy for each other with the exception of the intolerable Wilbur, whose success at poker had been so rudely interrupted.

'Gee,' said Wilbur, 'I guess I could work out where we stood in that game and how much I had won.'

'No,' said Lord Frederick, 'Where the game is interrupted by some disaster, like an earthquake, the gains and losses are all cancelled. After all, we don't know how it would have ended. The situation is covered by a rule issued by the Portland Club.'

'I never heard of such a rule,' said Wilbur sulkily, 'and I know darn well how the game was going to end. I never lose, do I, Pop?'

'Sure, son, but I guess we should accept Lord Frederick's ruling. He's our host, you see, and he wasn't playing.'

After another twenty minutes or so Wilbur remarked that Colonel McVane was taking a long time over fetching the police. At that point Jeeves, who was within earshot intervened in a way we must surely admire. So far we may think that his gangster act was no more than a normal reaction and just what we should ourselves have done in his place. His real genius revealed itself in the sequel and this was probably the first occasion when his genius was revealed at all. Admitting that he had chanced to hear the younger Mr Schwartz's remark, he apologized for speaking out of turn but felt that he had no alternative.

'Lord Frederick, I beg to suggest, with all due deference, that you and your guests might be wrong to await the return of Colonel McVane and wrong indeed to expect the arrival of the police. I happen to know that Colonel McVane had a reputation on the North-West Frontier as a skilled tracker, an exceptional marksman and a ruthless opponent. It was said of him, as of the Canadian Mounted Police, that he always got his man. No single tribesman he had singled out for death was ever known to escape. The petty thief who recently robbed your guests, Lord Frederick, made the mistake of his lifetime in pointing his weapon at the Colonel. Police action must now be the least of the criminal's worries and a prison would at least offer him a measure of safety. Should it be necessary to track this man down to the ends of the world, the Colonel will do it. I submit, Lord Frederick, that this small time gangster will never be seen again alive.'

Bowing to all present, Jeeves withdrew amidst words of thanks and looks of admiration, and we may fairly conclude that this moment was a turning point in his life. He had found that his keenest pleasure lay in resolving a situation and being regarded by everyone, for a moment, as a genius. The comment 'Isn't Jeeves marvellous!' (whether spoken or implied) was reward enough for his thought and effort. He wanted no more of life but it was essential that the final scene should be good. He himself must be expressionless, imperturbable, dignified and conclusively right. All other members of the cast must be horrified, confused, puzzled, and then finally should have the neat solution handed to them on a salver. At that point the curtain should fall, marking the end of the play. In this instance, however, there was a further sequel; a moment, as it were, when the leading player took his curtain call.

'I never heard,' said Lord Frederick afterwards, 'that Colonel McVane had fought on the North-West Frontier. Tell me, Jeeves, how you came to know about it.'

'I must confess, Lord Frederick, that I may have been guilty of exaggeration. The Colonel served with credit, I understand, in the Royal Army Ordnance Corps and was awarded the MBE on retirement. He was never stationed in India but had one turn of duty in British Honduras. The lies that I have told are like their father that begets them, gross as a mountain, open, palpable. Perhaps you might advise the Colonel to keep out of sight until our recent guests have left Monte Carlo?'

Lord Frederick Ranelagh now resumed his ordinary pattern of life, offering entertainment to his American friends and making a modest living without excessive effort. It must be confessed that his abilities, like his means, were limited. He was soon afterwards put to the proof in a still more painful fashion. It all began with the arrival at the Hermitage of the Bishop of Bongo Bongo. Readers will readily believe that there are many cheaper hotels than the Hermitage, not a few of them in Monte Carlo itself. Among the folk who circulate in its famous glass domed vestibule, colonial bishops are more the exception than the rule. If they frequent Monte Carlo at all it is to be surmised that they must usually stay somewhere else. But here he was, the Rt. Rev. Matthew Postlethwaite, DD and the credit manager assumed hopefully that his wife, who was with him, had private means. She was a lady of some distinction who looked about her with a certain disdain.

As time went on, however, the manager noted with concern that Monte Carlo seemed to be having the wrong effect on his lordship. He had been an impressive figure when he arrived, tallish, grey-haired and tropically bronzed. After a day or two he had discarded his clerical attire and was to be seen in white flannels and blazer. He was seen, moreover, in the bar. That he was heard to tell unseemly stories is quite untrue. That limerick about the young lady of Wantage was told, we believe, by someone else in the party, the Bishop capping it with the relatively innocuous man of Tralee. It would be true to say that he was desperately trying to look like a man of the world. The effort was visible, however, and it would take a seasoned traveller no more than ten minutes to realize that his new acquaintance was really a Bishop. By the end of the week the Bishop was seen, without his wife, at the casino, which is a mere five minutes walk from the Hermitage. For a day or so he looked more cheerful than usual. Then he began to look depressed. He turned a brave face to the world, mind you, and was evidently confident that tomorrow would be his lucky day. It would seem, however, that it wasn't, for his forced look of optimism was now painful to see. His wife had long since retired to bed with a daily headache and he had been left too much to himself. When he finally confided in someone, the confidant he chose was, of all people, Lord Frederick Ranelagh; not a guest of the hotel but one whose business sometimes brought him to the terrace or the bar. The lounge was almost deserted when the Bishop took Lord Frederick aside and made his desperate appeal for help.

'I was never in a casino before and can't imagine what came over me... You can imagine what shame I feel...

for a clergyman, for a bishop, to yield to this sort of temptation is sheer madness. I've learned my lesson but at what a price! As Oscar Wilde said "Experience is the name everyone gives to his mistakes." Well, I have paid mine and the price is heavy. I don't have the money to pay my hotel bill or travel back to London. I don't mean that I am destitute. Once in England I can raise the needed sum easily enough. I have some shares in a building society. I have some antique furniture in store. But here in Monte Carlo . . . It is terrible. I daren't even tell my wife, who is poorly and for whom the shock might prove too much . . . I have even had wicked thoughts of suicide . . . Could you possibly help me?'

'How much do you need?'

'Four hundred pounds would be enough.'

'What security can you offer?'

'Well, I did think of that. It so happens that my wife has a rather valuable bracelet, emeralds and sapphires, inherited from her mother and worth at least a thousand pounds. I borrowed it while she was asleep, heaven forgive me! I could leave it with it with you as security. You would be repaid in about two or three weeks' time.'

'But why don't you pawn it yourself?'

'I could never bring myself to do such a thing. I should die of shame. I really would.'

'I see. Very well, then. I'll tell you what I can do. First, I'll take this bracelet round to a jeweller friend of mine – his shop is just round the corner – and he'll tell me what it is actually worth. Second, I'll come back and tell you what he says. Third, if it is worth more than £600, I'll write you a cheque for £400. Fourth, you will send me a cheque for £500, after which (when it is cashed) I shall post the bracelet back to you. That's my best offer and you can take it or leave it.'

'It is very, very kind of you. Don't think I am ungrateful but I daren't accept your cheque. It would become known. People would think – more, they would know – that I had come to you for charity. I should feel more disgraced than I do now. It would have to be in cash.'

'Very well, then. But for a cash loan I should want £550. It would still be far below the market rate.'

'Agreed, my dear Lord Frederick. Here is the bracelet in its case.' He produced a black leather case from his pocket and opened it.

The bracelet sparkled impressively and Lord Frederick muttered 'It looks all right.'

'I can assure you,' said the Bishop, 'it is worth all and more than I have said. When satisfied on that point, you can cash a cheque at the bank and meet me back here in half an hour. I can't tell you how relieved I shall be when I know that my hotel bill can be paid. What a lesson it has been for me! What a fool I have been! How fortunate I am to find a good Samaritan, a man as generous and trusting as you have proved to be!'

The bracelet was quite as valuable as the Bishop had said and Lord Frederick came back with the money in cash. He placed the jewel case on a table and the Bishop checked that the bracelet was still there. Then he spent some time in counting the notes. Finally, Lord Frederick gave the Bishop a receipt for the bracelet and the Bishop gave Lord Frederick a receipt for the money. They shook hands on the bargain and Lord Frederick went back to his yacht well satisfied with the afternoon's work. He told Jeeves about it who looked rather grave.

'Might I see the bracelet, Lord Frederick?' he asked. The black leather case, when opened, proved to be empty. It was plainly a duplicate case which had been swapped for the real one while Lord Frederick was writing out his receipt. The hotel, when telephoned, reported that the Bishop and his wife had gone without paying their bill. A quick reference to *Who's Who* showed that there was indeed a Bishop of Bongo Bongo but he appeared to be an African called Nojarbawee, educated at a mission school and afterwards at Balliol College, Oxford. It was clear, in short, that Lord Frederick had been swindled. After making some inquiries, Jeeves was able, moreover, to report that the bogus Bishop was a well-known confidence man called Soapy Sid. He sometimes appeared as an aged Field-Marshal, often as a retired Ambassador, and not infrequently as an Archdeacon or Canon. His wife was his accomplice and they had both been in prison for fraud and false pretences. The bracelet had been stolen from another guest at the same hotel. It is a human instinct, when one is cheated, to recoup the loss as best one can, not always honestly. It is in this way that some people drift into a life of actual crime. Lord Frederick Ranelagh felt no such temptation but he did think at once about winning money at poker. This was, after all, a part of his way of life and no one could call it illegal.

Unfortunately for his plan, Colonel McVane was still on holiday, not out of idleness but because the Lowell's cabin cruiser was still in the harbour, a fact which prevented his return. Without McVane the dinner parties were difficult to organize, – which is how Lord Frederick came to visit the Hermitage in person at the time of the bogus bishop's departure. Without McVane the poker games could easily produce an actual deficit. What seems odd, in retrospect, is that Lord Frederick thought himself an ace player, which he actually was not. It was the Colonel whose game was above average, although well below the level reached by young Wilbur Schwartz. It was the Colonel who made the killing, on occasion, which certainly looked better than it would have done had the consistent winner been the host. But while Lord F. left the Colonel to win he had somehow convinced himself that he was himself the better player.

He now boldly invited men to visit the *Vortex II* and would seem to have done well enough against novice opponents. It was only a question of time, however, before he must run into trouble.

He met his Waterloo, in fact, when he threw a careless invitation to Mr Montague Todd. Had the name been Sir Jasper Todd,* Lord F. would have seen the danger, but this was Sir Jasper's younger brother, a man of whom his lordship had never heard. The stag dinner party went off well and Lord F. was rash enough to tell his guests of the recent incident in which Jeeves had saved him from what would have been indecent assault. He told this story when Jeeves was out of the room and Mr Todd showed great interest, remarking that Jeeves must be a useful man to have around. Lord F. agreed that he was, indeed, he was. The talk ended soon afterwards and the card game began. The details of play are not germane to the issue but Mr Todd's pile of chips rose higher and higher, Lord Frederick's dwindled to nothing. The point came when he had to admit that his gambling debt exceeded all the money he possessed. The other men round the table looked grave and one of them suggested that he might care to stake his yacht.†

'Where should I live?' asked the wretched Lord F.

---

* Sir Jasper Todd was at this time a well-known and successful speculator in real estate, especially in London. He has already been mentioned in this book (Vide supra, p. 20) as Chairman of the Barren Bogland Development Company, the failure of which brought loss to Mr Esmond Haddock of Deverill Hall. As regards his other interests Vide infra, p. 93.

† The *Vortex II* is no longer to be seen at Monte Carlo. Lord Frederick's fortunes deteriorated further during the following years and his yacht was eventually lost at sea in circumstances which attracted some adverse comment at the time. She had been heavily insured, she had no means of propulsion and sank in deep water without any prior stranding or collision. It was also shown that Lord Frederick had previously booked his hotel accommodation ashore. No insurance was paid and Lord F. is now a high official in the employ of the Race Relations Board.

'He lost the engines in another game last year . . .' another muttered somewhat unfeelingly.

'What about that racehorse Ranaloss?' said someone else, only to be told that it had broken its leg and had to be put down.

After a minute of embarrassed silence, Mr Todd caused a sensation when he said, 'What about Jeeves?'

'Well what about Jeeves?' asked Lord F. petulantly.

'You could stake him at an agreed valuation.'

'Good god! But I can't compel him to enter your service! The man is beyond price anyway!'

'You can sack him – and I should have thought that you needed to do that anyway. Then you can tell him of my offer, fifty per cent more than his present wage.'

'If I lose him I shall expect you to cancel what else I owe you.'

'Agreed. I place on the table my cigarette lighter, representing Jeeves. That is Lord Frederick's stake. Tony, the buck is with you.'

The game was resumed. Readers should recall that poker, unlike many other card games, is a game not of luck but of skill. Had Lord F. studied Major Hoffman's classic book on the game? He probably had but the game requires some innate qualities in addition. The successful player must have a mathematical and calculating brain. He must have a cool presence of mind, a mental alertness, some psychological insight and an expressionless face. Did Lord F. have any or all of these advantages? He had, in fact, none of them. Mr Todd, by contrast, was a man for whose convenience the game might have been invented. The result was inevitable and the moment came when Lord Frederick stared at the cards and whispered in a stricken voice, 'I've lost Jeeves.'

The party broke up and his lordship spent a sleepless

night. He felt all too much like one who is to be shot at dawn and who wonders, as many such a victim must wonder, why it could not be done at a more reasonable hour.

Lord Frederick sent for Jeeves after breakfast. 'I regret to say that I lost heavily at cards last night. I lost pretty well all I have. The result is that I must cut down on my domestic staff. With infinite regret I have decided, for the time being, to do without a valet. This moment would be even more painful for me if I could not tell you at the same time of another place that is offered you at a higher wage. When I told Mr Todd of my financial predicament, he said at once that he would be glad to have you in his service. May I tell him that you will accept?'

'I appreciate your tact, Lord Frederick, and will accept the offer. I realize indeed that it would be awkward if I didn't. You need not, however, have invented a story. I was on deck last night and watched your game through the skylight, which was open, allowing me to hear much of what was said. I could have played your hand better than you did, Lord Frederick. Now that I am to leave your service, I would add that I should have valued myself at a rather higher price; higher at least than the cost of a cigarette lighter.'

Chapter 6

The Detectives

To achieve eminence in the dignified profession of being a gentleman's gentleman depends, in the first place, upon the employer being, in fact, a gentleman. Any failure in this respect must prevent the g's g. from reaching first base (whatever that may mean). This is where many an otherwise beautiful relationship comes unstuck and the instance of Mr Montague Todd is a case in point. On the more superficial level Mr Todd might be said to pass muster. He was aged about thirty-five, fair-haired, slim, of medium height, clean-shaven, and generally presentable. He was able to make the correct responses in any unexacting conversation. It was when inspecting Mr Todd's wardrobe that Jeeves's heart began to sink.

Mr Todd had a second-floor suite at the Pan-americana Hotel and the cupboard space, which was ample and lined in polished hardboard, contained all the clothes which any valet could expect to find. The suits were expensive and came from Saville Row but the patterns were too loud, the cut too flashy, the colours too hot and the result too awful. The shirts were individually tailored in Jermyn Street, the ties were in woven silk, the socks from the Burlington arcade and the shoes from McPhee, but the total effect was mere disaster. After infinite expense and care, Mr Todd looked like something the cat had brought in – a cat, moreover, with an outstanding lack of discrimination. Nor could Jeeves do anything to educate his employer, all his hints being merely ignored. To brush and press so many unsuitable garments was, for Jeeves, an agony in itself, but his sufferings did not end there. Unseemly as Mr Todd might appear, he had friends even less fit to be seen. Chief of these was a solicitor called Cedric Snodgrass, a dark-clad figure of rather seedy appearance with a soup-stained drooping grey moustache. There is no such name as Cedric, as Jeeves well knew (the misnomer resulting from a printer's error in a novel by Sir Walter Scott) and the distrust aroused by such a non-existent word is inevitable. But Mr Snodgrass's furtive manner made things worse. He was evidently Mr Todd's financial mentor but with functions limited to business. For more social purposes Mr Todd relied upon the boon companionship of Tony O'Keefe and Gus Quiggin, prosperous young men of boisterous manner and deplorable costume. On more intimate occasions Mr Todd could rely upon the sprightly effervescence of Miss Fanny Fotheringay, an actress said to be resting between her engagements in the West End. His other acquaintances were birds of passage, transient poker players and people generally, it would seem, with money to lose.

One thing apparent from the outset was that Montague Todd was not his own master. Granted that he might make some money on the side, he lived essentially on an allowance from his brother, Sir Jasper, the former London property tycoon. Sir Jasper had an office in Monaco, some building projects along the coast and good reason to have his appointed agent in the vicinity. His brother was that agent, at least for some purposes, but Snodgrass had an even more confidential role, nor would it surprise anyone to learn that Snodgrass was watched in turn by someone else. Had Sir Jasper trusted anyone in the world (a doubtful point) his younger brother was not the man in whom he would have chosen to confide. For Montague, loyal or otherwise, had no more than average ability and rather less than average application to the work in hand. As for Jeeves, he looked upon his employer's circle of friends with quiet distaste. It would be wrong to say that he had exceptionally high moral principles. He had thus seen little to deplore in Lord Frederick's way of life for Lord F. had style. Jeeves's insistence was rather on social standards, correct appearance and polite behaviour; on all the graces which Mr Todd so conspicuously lacked.

At this time the members of the Junior Ganymede Club in Monte Carlo numbered about nine, not enough to form a local branch but enough to justify a weekly gathering at the Café Florentine in the Rue Suffren Reymond. It was in this congenial and well-informed circle that Jeeves came to hear about Sir Jasper's all but criminal transactions for which he was so well known in the City. Old Tom Atwell, valet to a Lord of Appeal, warned him against being associated with the Todds.

'One day,' he said solemnly, 'they'll go too far and you'll find yourself in court, a witness, maybe a suspect, perhaps an accessory after the fact. If things were to go badly, you would never have another appointment in any family of consequence. Leave these people, Jeeves, before it is too late!'

Jeeves agreed that his employer might well end in

prison but insisted that his worst offences were not criminal but aesthetic.

'To begin with,' he explained, 'Mr Todd uses Glisteroll on his hair. It is the sort of stuff used by yokels on market day.'

'That is not quite true,' Atwell objected, 'I have known gentlemen who have used Glisteroll; not many, I'll admit, but two or three.'

'But he also uses Dazzlo toothpaste, which smells of aniseed!'

'Ah, that is a more serious matter. Dazzlo is strictly for working-class Italians. No gentleman *ever* uses Dazzlo. About that there can be no argument at all.'

'But there is worse to follow, Mr Atwell! Mr Todd also uses Seductor Aftershave Lotion!'

'Not really? Enough, Mr Jeeves! Seductor on top of Dazzlo? The mind recoils from such a disgusting combination. This is not to be endured! You should leave this man's service at once!'

Faced with appalling clothes and revolting smells, Jeeves would have resigned, no doubt, at an early date but an event was to take place which would save him from making that decision. On a fine morning in June and at the usual hour, Jeeves came to Mr Todd's bedroom, drew the curtains and wished his master good morning. There was no reply, a fact easily explained in that Mr Todd was not there. The bed, which had been occupied, was empty, so was the adjacent bathroom and so was the rest of the suite. Mr Todd had vanished and his absence was accounted for by a note pinned neatly to the pillow.

Written in block capitals on the back of yesterday's luncheon menu, it read as follows:–

MONTAGUE TODD IS THE PRISONER
OF THE YOUNG LEVELLERS LIBERATION

ARMY AND WILL ~~ONLY~~ BE RELEASED
ONLY ON RECEIPT OF £500,000 PAYABLE
INTO ACCOUNT No. 53726449 AT THE
SUPRANATIONAL BANK, GENEVA,
FAILING WHICH PAYMENT BY NOON ON
FRIDAY 21st JUNE HE WILL BE EXECUTED
AS AN ENEMY OF THE PEOPLE

Having read some detective fiction, Jeeves touched
nothing in the suite and, from the hotel reception desk,
telephoned the hotel manager, the Chief of Police and
Mr Snodgrass. So useful did he make himself that he
was allowed to be present at the conference which presently took place in Mr Todd's suite.

'But the situation is incredible!' said the red-faced and
portly manager. 'Mr Todd came into the hotel at 1.30 am,
as the night porter assures us, saying goodnight to Mr
O'Keefe in whose car he arrived and who is a witness to
his arrival. He was gone by 8.0am taking only his
pyjamas. Nobody left the hotel between 1.30 and 8.0. We
have searched the hotel and there is no sign of him
anywhere. There is no trace of a struggle, no proof that he
offered any resistance. No one saw or heard anything
suspicious and I, for one, cannot imagine how the kidnapping can have taken place.'

'He was dragged through a window and carried down
a ladder?' suggested Mr Snodgrass.

'Impossible!' said the manager, 'Look for yourself!
This suite has an iron grille outside each window in the
Spanish style – the Dictator of Patagonia was staying in
this suite last year and the ironwork was installed at his
insistence.'

'That is the least of it!' added the Chief of Police.
'General Bastante Nervioso of Bolivia is staying here
now and asked yesterday for police protection. Detec-

tives were watching the hotel all night, and had nothing
to report.'

'And he didn't even take his dressing-gown?' asked
the manager.

Jeeves opened the wardrobe and pointed silently and
sadly to a purple and gold monstrosity. 'It is still there,'
he said with a sigh. 'And so is his passport, his driving
licence and his American Express credit card.'

'What if he is not to be found?' asked the Chief of
Police. 'Will the ransom be paid?'

'I have telephoned Sir Jasper Todd,' replied Snodgrass, 'and I know, in any case, that he is insured against
kidnapping. The policy covers all members of his family, his brother included.'

'But what action is he taking?' asked the manager.

'He is sending his own representative to investigate;
the famous Mr Hercule Poirot. It so happens that he is
on holiday at Antibes. He should be here before midday
and may well have solved the problem before nightfall.'

'The police have no need of amateur help,' said the
Chief rather sharply.

'Ah, but you must see that Sir Jasper's problem is not
the same as yours,' said Snodgrass placatingly. 'Your
task is to find the criminal. Sir Jasper has to decide
whether to pay a ransom. You and Poirot have to consider the same facts but not from exactly the same angle.
You probably know already who the criminals are and
need only find the evidence on which to convict.'

'As you say, Monsieur. To know is one thing. To
prove what you know is something else!'

The meeting broke up without anyone reaching any
useful conclusion. Mr Todd had vanished and no one
knew how. His car was still in the hotel garage, his
money was still in his wallet, his sun-glasses still on his
dressing-table. He was gone and persons unknown
claimed to hold him captive. In what direction should

the pursuit go? What other building, the hotel apart, should be searched? Who else was there to question? The detectives did their best to look purposeful and alert but their inquiries led nowhere. They were faced by a seemingly insoluble problem.

Chapter 7

The Villain Unmasked

In some parts of this biography the author has been driven to invent the conversation which must have taken place. In others he has done no more than give the general purport of what was said. On the subject, however, of the crime we have now to analyse we have a wealth of detailed evidence, journalistic, forensic and (eventually) reminiscent. We can rely, moreover, on the autobiography published by the hotel manager, M. Jean Delacroix, *The Memoirs of an Innkeeper,* for which these events provide the crisis of his otherwise dull career. We learn from him, for example, that Hercule Poirot was small with an egg-shaped head, with a large moustache of military aspect and with eagle eyes which took in every detail of what he saw. Still more to the point we have from him an almost verbatim account of the first interview which took place with Mr Cedric Snodgrass, Mr Tony O'Keefe, Jeeves and the manager himself. Monsieur Poirot impressed the others by coming at once to the essential point.

'You will realize, Monsieur Snodgrass, that I have been instructed only by long-distance telephone. I 'ave not the personal rapport with Sir Jasper Todd. I never 'eard before of the man who is missing. So my first question is simple. Can the ransom, if necessary, be paid?'

'I am violating no confidence, Monsieur Poirot, when I assure you that Sir Jasper is a man of substantial wealth. To pay such a sum as this would cause him no more than a passing inconvenience. I have also reason to know that he is heavily insured against this form of blackmail.'

'So that he could pay an even larger sum, is it not?'

'Undoubtedly. For his wife, son or daughter he – or the underwriters – would pay as much again.'

'So one might consider this £500,000 as a modest demand, exactly calculated, as much as a younger brother is worth?'

'That is so, Monsieur Poirot. The amount is nicely adjusted, less than would be paid for a daughter; more, much more, than anyone would pay for an aunt.'

'Would I be right in supposing that Mr Montague Todd is himself unable to pay that ransom?'

'I may say in confidence, Monsieur Poirot, that his own fortune is negligible.'

'So the criminals we are to deal with have been skilful in fixing their price. The next point of interest is the demand note. There is no such organization as the Young Levellers Liberation Army, nor if there were, would they have written a note like that. No, that would not be possible.'

'Why not?' asked Mr O'Keefe bluntly.

'Observe, my friend, the words used. The author began by writing "WILL ONLY BE RELEASED" and then realized that this would be ungrammatical. So he changed the sentence to read "WILL BE RELEASED ONLY ON RECEIPT OF . . ." Are we expected to believe that "Young Levellers" wrote that – mere university students, people we know to be practically illiterate? No, we are up against real criminals.'

'But why should they pretend to be young revolutionaries?' asked M. Delacroix.

'To make their threat more convincing,' replied Poirot. 'If they are liberal idealists, lovers of humanity, they will be ready to murder anyone. But they are better educated than that and one of them we might even think a little pedantic.'

'They are professional, you think?' asked Mr Snodgrass.

'Beyond question, Monsieur! Beyond all shadow of doubt! Consider what they would seem to have done! A group of them have soundlessly entered a hotel which is locked, barred, guarded and watched. They have passed the night porter, an ex sous-officier of an integrity which is absolute. They have kidnapped a guest and taken him out of the hotel in his pyjamas, without so much as his dressing-gown or overcoat. Their victim may die of pneumonia on the second day of his captivity but the total effort is well beyond the abilities of any high-minded people who are working for the good of mankind. Our own brain cells must exercise themselves on this case. We have to deal with people who have brains!'

'You will need time, Monsieur Piorot, to examine the room at leisure?' suggested Delacroix.

'No, Monsieur, I have already done so. The one important fact was obvious to me in the first two minutes!'

'And what was that?' gasped Snodgrass.

'I could see from the bathroom shelf that Mr Todd uses Glisteroll on his hair (a revolting habit). There is no trace of that on the pillow. So we can be certain that Mr Todd never spent the night there. He was kidnapped at an earlier hour. The man who entered the hotel at 1.30 was someone else.'

'But you forget, Monsieur Poirot, that I saw him enter the hotel!' O'Keefe's protest was emphatic and almost shrill.

'Tell us the circumstances, Mr O'Keefe.'

'We had been at the cabaret, "The Birds of Paradise" – Todd, Gus Quiggin and I – but we were disappointed in the show, the star performer being absent, and came away early. I drove Monty to this hotel and said good-bye to him on the doorstep.'

'And your companion could not have been someone else impersonating Mr Todd?'

'Good grief, no! He chatted quite a bit, talked of people we had recently met, remembered events we both knew about. It was Monty all right and I could take my oath on it.'

Hercule Poirot looked crestfallen but presently had another idea.

'Look, Mr O'Keefe, I wonder if I might ask you to perform a delicate mission – one that may be vital to my investigation? Could you find out for me – tactfully, you will understand – where Miss Fotheringay was on the night of the crime?'

O'Keefe agreed readily enough and went on his way, at which point Snodgrass asked Poirot what Miss Fotheringay had to do with the kidnapping.

'Nothing at all!' said Poirot promptly. But I wanted to get rid of O'Keefe. He is clearly an accessory to the crime and I reject his evidence completely!'

'And what do you conclude from that?' asked Snodgrass.

'My conclusion, my friend, is that Mr Todd has been kidnapped by a highly professional gang. Our chances of finding him are remote. I shall advise Sir Jasper to pay the ransom.'

'But what if the underwriters take a different view?' asked Snodgrass, 'I have this moment received a telegram, telling me that they have engaged Lord Peter Wimsey to represent their interests. He is on holiday, it seems, at Port Grimaud* and will be with us later this evening. He will look at the matter, I suspect, from a different point of view.'

'His amateur blundering should at least afford us some amusement. He does not realize, perhaps, that I, Hercule Poirot, am already on the case!'

From the sequel it might be guessed that Lord Peter was, in fact, well aware of Poirot's presence. The speed with which his sports car covered the distance must command the admiration of all who know the traffic conditions on the Côte d'Azur. He was not in time for dinner, to be sure, but the kitchen was still able to provide him and his faithful man Bunter with soup and sandwiches. Snodgrass told him, meanwhile, what the situation was and to what conclusions Hercule Poirot had been led. While very much aware of each other's activity it is noteworthy that these great men never actually met. To Snodgrass, Lord Peter Wimsey's appearance came as an unpleasant surprise. He knew of Wimsey's reputation as a private detective and expected him to look the part. He was taken aback by the man who appeared, a character of foppish appearance with straw-coloured hair brushed back from his forehead,

---

* Port Grimaud is a recently constructed yachtsman's paradise in the Gulf of St. Tropez, more Provencal in style than any more genuinely antique village on the Côte d'Azur. It is generally assumed (perhaps wrongly) that only Germans can afford to live or stay there; the Arabs having no interest in yachts. Wimsey, as we know from the French press, was a guest at this time of the Graf von Sauerkraut, whose gourmet table he quitted with some regret.

with an ugly nose and a faintly foolish smile. Still less impressive was his habit of ending a sentence with 'eh?' or 'what?' and concluding a conversation with 'right-ho!' As a stage character man–about–town his manner might have been thought over-acted. As against that, there *are* people who say 'what?' and Wimsey was undoubtedly one of them. The habit may be dated but is not actually illegal. It would be interesting, at least, to learn that he discarded Poirot's theory at the outset, having found one of his own. On the contrary, as it turned out, he treated Poirot's theory with respect. On the day after Wimsey's arrival Delacroix held another meeting in Mr Todd's suite, attended only by Snodgrass, by Bunter and Jeeves and (at Wimsey's suggestion) by Miss Fanny Fotheringay. Wimsey had already had separate interviews with Tony O'Keefe and Gus Quiggin and had arranged to meet them again that evening. Miss Fotheringay turned out to be an attractive brunette with a genuine career as an actress and only a passing interest in Montague Todd. By a few telephone inquiries Wimsey had established the fact that she was perfectly well-known to London theatrical agents and that her character, as apart from her morals, was unblemished.

'It's jolly good of you all to come along,' said Wimsey. 'I hope it wasn't shockingly inconvenient and all that. I just want to get a picture, don't you know, of what happened. Mr O'Keefe and Mr Quiggin have been most helpful – jolly decent, in fact – and it would seem that Mr Todd was at a carbaret called "The Birds of Paradise". With him were his friends Mr O'Keefe and Mr Quiggin and the three of them had supper together. At about eleven they were joined by you, Miss Fotheringay, and you all four watched the first act of the floor show. Was it any good?'

'The girls were pretty but the star of the show, Olga

Orloff, the fan dancer,* had a bad cold and her under-study was a poor substitute.'

'A bad cold, poor dear? I don't wonder, do you? It always seems a bit chilly, doesn't it? So you decided not to wait for Act Two, eh? When did you leave?'

'At about one or a quarter past. But we separated in the car park. Monty and Tony were to go off in Tony's car. Gus took me in his Jaguar to show me his penthouse on the roof of the Fantasia building – the view from there is simply out of this world.'

'I can well believe it, Miss Fotheringay. Specially by moonlight, what? So Tony drives Monty to this hotel. Then, if we believe one theory that has been put for-ward, there is a lightning substitute. Monty goes off into captivity and someone else, disguised as Monty enters the hotel, comes into this room, hangs up his evening clothes, puts on his pyjamas and then vanishes into thin air. As a story, I find that a bit hard to swallow, somehow. Too many loose ends, what?'

'It's a load of rubbish,' said Fanny with spirit. 'It makes Tony a crook, a member of some gang, in a plot against old Monty. Well, he isn't! He may be a wild Irishman but he isn't that sort of criminal.'

'You think,' said Lord Peter Wimsey, quickly, 'that he is some other sort of criminal?'

'Well, you know what I mean. He'd smuggle any-thing past the customs. He's not a man from whom to buy a racehorse or a second-hand Bentley. But for actual crime he hasn't the nerve and hasn't the brain. Gus I'll

---

* For readers unfamiliar with this form of entertainment it should be explained that a fan dancer is a young lady of attractive appearance whose sole attire on stage consists of two good-sized feather fans, one in each hand. Her art is to move around while adjusting the feathers so as to provide a measure of decency which is never quite consistent or complete. The occupational risk of catching cold is obvious. Olga Orloff is men-tioned frequently in memoirs of her period, especially in *Stage Door Johnny* by John Rashway, whose third wife she eventually became.

admit is a different sort of character. I wouldn't say but what Gus might pull a fast one; but he has an alibi.'

'Is Quiggin his real name?'

'I guess so. You wouldn't call yourself Quiggin for choice, would you? Not if your real name was Featherstonehaugh or Grosvenor?'

'I see what you mean. As against that, you might conclude that other people would accept the name more readily, using the argument you have just put forward.'

In two other interviews that evening Lord Peter convinced himself that what Fanny said about O'Keefe and Quiggin was pretty near the truth. If there was a plot, Quiggin could have planned it but O'Keefe was not the man to carry it out. Quiggin had served in the army, by his own account, and came, so he said, from the Isle of Man. That both these claims were false became apparent in a matter of minutes:

'In the infantry, eh?' asked Lord Peter cheerfully. 'In what regiment?'

'The Royal Fusiliers.'

'Jolly good show. Let's see, what is their number in the line? Stupid of me – I ought to know.'

'The fifth, formed by Charles II.'

'So you always drink the loyal toast?'

'But of course.'

'And where do you come from in the Isle of Man?'

'From Ramsey.'

'In the south, near Castletown?'

'That's right.'

'And do remind me – what are the judges called in the Isle of Man?'

'Why – Judges, no I mean, Justices.'

'Of course – silly of me to have forgotten. A most attractive island – I'll have to go there again some day.'

When Mr Quiggin had gone, Lord Peter Wimsey

called Bunter in from the next room and asked him whether he had taken all the required photographs.

'Yes, my lord. And was your lordship satisfied with Mr Quiggin's account of himself?'

'No, Bunter, the man is bogus. The Royal Fusiliers are the seventh of the line, formed by James II (as every schoolboy should know) in 1685. They never drink the loyal toast – King William IV excused them, saying that their loyalty was beyond question. Ramsey is in the north of the Isle of Man, where the two judges are called Deemsters. No, Mr Quiggin is not what he purports to be.'

'To me, my lord, he looks rather like Robert Quiller, who played a part in that McClelland kidnapping case.'

'I remember it. The young McClelland connived at his own kidnapping and shared in the ransom which his grandfather paid. And that – damn it, yes – that is what Montague Todd has done! This man Quiller – and I do believe he is the same – put him up to it. Todd and O'Keefe are in it together and Quiggin planned it.'

'We still don't know exactly what happened, my lord. We don't know where Todd is hiding.'

'No we don't, Bunter, but I know enough to advise the underwriters not to pay anything to the Levellers Liberation Army. I shall state my opinion that Mr Todd is in no danger.'*

That Lord Peter Wimsey had so advised became public knowledge in a matter of days with the unexpected result that there was a new demand for ransom, posted to Mr Snodgrass in a letter with a Villefranche postmark:

---

* This whole incident is described in a biography of Lord Peter Wimsey called *Whimsical Sleuth* by Wallace Edgar (See Chap. 23), written and published against his lordship's wishes. The narrative is highly suspect and the main conclusions relating to this affair are obviously incorrect.

MONTAGUE TODD IS STILL A PRISONER UNDER SENTENCE OF DEATH. THE RANSOM OF £500,000 SHOULD NOW BE PAID INTO ACCOUNT No. 5461833175 AT THE CREDIT UNIVERSAL AT BERNE, FAILING WHICH PAYMENT HE WILL BE EXECUTED ON FRIDAY 28th JUNE, AT NOON.

Lord Peter Wimsey was about to leave Monte Carlo when this new demand came. He had no difficulty in deciding that the recipient of the ransom, if the under-writers were to pay it, would be Sir Jasper Todd him-self. He was not a man to stand idly by while any chance of profit remained.

Hercule Poirot had gone his way and Lord Peter Wimsey was no longer on the scene. Still present and still worried was the hotel manager, Jean Delacroix, who felt that something terrible had happened, that a guest at his hotel had been kidnapped and that the mystery had never been solved. For all he knew, it could happen again. A devout catholic, he confessed his fears to Father Lagrange for whose advice he had often been grateful in the past.

'It so happens, my son, that we have here at the Convalescent Home of the Redemption an English priest who is recovering from an illnesss – from jaun-dice, I believe – and who has a great reputation for elucidating mysteries which are beyond the skill of the police. It is my own private belief that a little puzzle like this would actually hasten his recovery. Father Brown is known to me only by reputation but I really think he might solve your problem.'

Jean Delacroix was a little disappointed, however, when he met Father Brown for the first time. The little English priest was round-faced, unimpressive, pale, clumsy innocent and apparently simple. He gazed round at the suite from which Montague Todd had vanished and listened carefully to all the relevant facts. How on earth could he be expected to succeed where Poirot and Wimsey had been at least partly baffled? What truth could he find which had been hidden from them?

The little priest blinked about him uncertainly and finally addressed his first question to Jeeves: 'These friends of Mr Todd, the people who were with him on the evening he disappeared – are they of evil character?'

'No, sir,' replied Jeeves promptly. 'I mean no, father,' (he corrected himself). 'They live, as it were, for pleasure, and their behaviour would not commend itself to everyone. But there is no real harm in them.'

'You would know, of course, if they were criminals?'

'Naturally, father.'

'But they would cheat the customs if they had the chance?'

'Of course, sir – father.'

'And cheating an insurance company is much the same thing?'

'It is usually thought so.'

'So it would not surprise you to learn that Mr Todd's kidnapping had been arranged between him and his friends?'

'Not really, sir.'

'But you don't know how it was managed?'

'No, sir.'

'Thank you, Jeeves.' Father Brown turned to the others and said, 'That settles the main question and I should suppose that the underwriters will refuse to pay up. But you still wonder, Monsieur Delacroix, what actually happened. Well I put myself, first of all, in Mr Todd's place, I want to disappear for a time. I want to vanish until the ransom has been paid. How do I set about it? How do I hide? I am a man of only moderate intelligence – isn't that right, Jeeves? (Jeeves nodded.) But I have a friend of greater ability and wider experience have I not? (Jeeves nodded again.) Left to myself, I should hide in a tent, in a cave, in some ruined building in the heart of a wooded area. But my friend advises me differently. Where do you hide a pebble? On the beach. Where do you hide a leaf? In the forest. Where do you hide a holidaymaker? In a hotel. And in which hotel among many? In the hotel from which he is missing. Why? Because inquiries will be made at all the *other* hotels. Now, Monsieur Delacroix, you have had sleepless nights, I know, asking yourself the same questions, again and again. Will you please repeat those questions now?'

'Of course. Well, I ask first how a complete stranger could pass himself off as Mr Todd, deceiving Mr O'Keefe, deceiving the night porter and obtaining the key of Mr Todd's suite.'

'No stranger did this. It was Mr Todd who entered the hotel at 1.30 – and no one else.'

'Who was it then who entered this room, hung up his evening clothes, put on his pyjamas and disturbed the bedclothes?'

'Mr Todd himself.'

'How then did he leave the hotel with the windows barred, the front door guarded, the building watched?'

'He did not leave!'

'Do you mean that he hid until morning, disguised himself and checked in next day under a different name?'

'I doubt if he acted as crudely as that. My guess is that he booked another room in advance, checked in some days before, acted as two guests for a short time, sleeping half the night in either bed, and then – on the night in question – left this room in his pyjamas and walked quietly to the other room he now occupies.'

'How are we to recognize him?'

'By opposites. Was Mr Todd fair?'

'Yes.'

'He is now dark. Was he clean-shaven?'

'Yes.'

'He now has a beard, a moustache or both. Was he slim?'

'Yes.'

'He will now be more rounded. Did he smoke?'

'No.'

'He will now be a smoker. Did he bathe in the pool?'

'I don't think so.'

'He will swim each day before breakfast. Do you begin to have a picture of the man?'

'No, father. But we have many guests, remember.'

At this point Jeeves intervened with a discreet cough.

'Excuse me, sir. I think I can identify the gentleman by this evening. May I call at your office at, say six o'clock?' True to his word Jeeves was punctual to the minute and came straight to the point: 'Good evening, sir. Mr Montague Todd is the guest resident in room No. 437. I no longer consider myself in his service.'

'But how did you come to know this?'

'Well, sir, a gentleman who adopts a disguise may change his clothes, his hair colour, his complexion and accent. Spinoza observes sir, that men govern nothing with more difficulty than their tongues, but here the philosopher is surely wrong. It is their habits they fail to govern. Having changed everything else, a man who assumes a disguise will probably retain the same toothpaste, hairwash and after-shave lotion. Mr Todd's tastes are peculiar, sir, for he prefers Glisteroll, Dazzlo and Seductor, products of which few real gentlemen would make use – and none, surely, would use all three. I asked the chambermaids to check in all bathrooms this afternoon and in only one of them did all three substances feature. I ventured, sir, to offer a small reward in your name. If you thought my own services deserve any recognition, sir, I should not refuse a sum equivalent to my fare back to London.'

Chapter 8

Bertie Wooster

With the publicity which centred upon the Todd Kidnapping Case (for which Montague Todd was jailed for two years) Jeeves gained his established repute as a man of the world. As from this time his advice was sought throughout Mayfair. It was this affair, moreover, which brought him the friendship of Lord Peter Wimsey's man, Bunter. They had been colleagues, momentarily, in Monte Carlo and each had learned to respect the other. It was now Jeeves who proposed Bunter for membership of the Junior Ganymede and it was Bunter who marked the occasion by offering Jeeves a useful piece of advice.

'You will have realized, Jeeves, that my master, Lord Peter Wimsey, is an extremely clever man?'

'Of that there can be no doubt at all.'

'He is clever, moreover, in a subtle way. There are people who act cleverly and then say "Look how clever I have been!" This is a mistake too often made by Frenchmen and sometimes by Germans. Lord Peter acts

in the opposite way. He is diffident beforehand and
confesses afterwards that it was a fluke. He leads people
into chattering unguardedly. By his very appearance he
sets a trap.'

'Yes, I see that,' said Jeeves. 'Father Brown plays the
same trick in a different way.'

'Just so, but hear my advice. Never accept service
with a gentleman who is as clever as that. Indeed I
would go further and suggest you avoid service with
anyone who is clever at all. I am loyal to Lord Peter and
take great interest in the criminal cases he chooses to
investigate. But for that I should have quitted his service
long ago. Imagine for yourself, Jeeves, an employer
whom you could never hope to deceive, someone who
sees through every excuse and knows every trick. I'll be
frank, Jeeves: it is not convenient at all. We have, after
all, our private lives to lead. Do we want an employer
who can tell where we have been from the clay on our
boots, from the blonde hairs on our jacket lapel, from
the smell of whisky on our breath? No, we want a little
privacy. So make your own choice now. Find the employer who meets your exact needs. He need not be
mentally handicapped but he should certainly be far
from clever. Think back, Jeeves, and tell me what you
have learnt so far in your years of service.'

Jeeves replied:

> ' "Myself when young did eagerly frequent
> Doctor and Saint, and heard great argument
> About it and about: but evermore
> Came out by the same door as in I went".'

'I don't believe you, Jeeves. You have learnt more
than that, but not from books.'

'Well, I learnt to beware of aunts, avoiding them as
much as I could. I learnt to move silently, hear every-

thing and say nothing. As page boy in an academy for young ladies, I learnt that all girls are to be avoided as much as possible and that those with red hair are especially dangerous. I learnt that the ideal employer must always be, and should always remain, a bachelor. I have learnt a great deal about flat racing. I came to realize that a gentleman's gentleman has a more interesting life than a butler. I discovered a certain talent for playing bridge; as also, later, for playing poker. From sad experience I came to the conclusion that a lover of Dumb Chums is an employer to avoid. Nor can I tolerate an employer who fails to dress as a gentleman should. I have lived on board my employer's yacht at Monte Carlo, an experience which was interesting in itself but which I do not wish to repeat. I have had some experience of crooks and I find that my preference is for prosperous and reasonably but not fanatically honest men. I have come to the conclusion, finally, that my employer must always be a gentleman.'

'In a nutshell, your employer must be a rich bachelor and one without a passion for horses, dogs, goldfish—'

'Or *parrots*.'

'Just so. He should dress and behave properly and enjoy, in every sense, the status of a gentleman. All that you have learnt by experience. Let me now insist that your employer should also be stupid: good-natured, popular, but utterly brainless.'

'Why is that so important?'

'Because he is thus dependent on you. Take my case now, it is just the other way round. I depend on Lord Peter, who is far cleverer than I can ever hope to be. I shall have to play second fiddle until death us do part.'

'I see what you mean. You are his Watson and he is your Holmes.'

'For ever. So plan your own life better. Don't wait

to see what vacancy offers. Choose beforehand the employer who will best serve your purpose.'

Impressed by this argument, Jeeves turned to the Junior Ganymede Club Book and spent hours – more than that, he spent days – in studying the biographies there pitilessly exposed. He browsed over names and nicknames, from Oofy Prosser to Catsmeat Pirbright, from Bingo Little to Gussie Fink-Nottle. For stupidity, at least, many of them seemed to qualify but some of them overdid it to the point of lunacy, Freddie Widgeon being a case in point, and he was probably a shade more intelligent than Barmy Phipps or Looney Coote. Some who were ideal in other respects were obviously penniless. Several of the more prosperous were a shade too clever, and some few were of insufficiently good family. After exhaustive research, Jeeves found himself turning back repeatedly to an entry under Section W.

NAME/TITLE: Wooster, Bertram Wilberforce (the surname pronounced as in Worcester Sauce)

FAMILY: Nephew of Sir George Wooster, Bart. heir to the Earldom of Yaxley. Has numerous other relations.

BORN: Date unknown. Early left an orphan and much under the influence of various aunts.

STATUS: Bachelor. Too much of a schoolboy for girls to take seriously.

INCOME: Ample, but includes an allowance from his Uncle Willoughby.

EDUCATED: Eton and Magdalen, Oxford.

ADDRESS: 6A Crighton Mansions, Berkeley Street, W1.

INTELLIGENCE: 2 (Maximum 10)

OTHER SERVANTS: None

HOBBIES: Golf, tennis, racquets.

VIRTUES: Well-meaning, generous, friendly, unsuspicious, anxious to make his friends happy.

FAILINGS: Occasionally drunk, weak-willed, easily

deceived, not remarkable for courage, lacking in common sense.

GENERAL: Lives in terror of his Aunt Agatha, but is on good terms with his Aunt Dahlia, who employs the inimitable cook, Anatole. He is a member of the Drones Club and was at school or college with several other members. He will always go to the help of a friend but often with disastrous results.

RECOMMENDATION: OK.   SIGNED: James Meadowes

Jeeves could not persuade himself that B.W. was the perfect employer but he already knew that no such creature exists. He thought, however, that Bertram was highly suitable and far too good for Meadowes, a member of the Club with whom he had so far had little contact. He now made up for this past neglect and saw to it one evening that Meadowes's glass was never empty for long. 'Bertram?' said Meadowes, 'He's a good chap, a good man to work for!'

'Why do you say that, Jim?'

'Cos he can't count. He doesn't know how many shirts he has or how many handkerchiefs. He doesn't miss a few and, luckily, we take the same size.'

'But I'll bet you daren't wear his socks.'

'You're right there, pal. Nor I daren't. But they vanish, you know, and I know where to sell 'em, the silk ones, anyway. Socks like these, now (he produced a pair, crimson with grey spots), these sell for quite a useful price.'

'Coo!' said Jeeves, 'I wouldn't mind having a pair of those! Tell you what! I'll give you double the price you normally ask. How's that for a deal?'

'Done, my friend, and good value at that. Remember to pick out the initial tag, though, the B.W.W. We don't want to have questions asked, do we?'

Later that evening, Jeeves put the socks into a large

envelope and inserted with them a note in block capitals, 'STOLEN BY YOUR MAN MEADOWES AND SOLD TO ME – A WELL-WISHER'. He then posted this envelope to Bertram W. Wooster, Esq. 6A Crighton Mansions, Berkeley Street, W1. Two days later he called at that address and asked whether Mr Wooster had a vacancy for a gentleman's personal gentleman. It seems that he had. Years afterwards Bertie Wooster was to describe the moment when Jeeves came into his life and the words he used were highly significant:

> '. . . Lots of people think I'm too dependent on him. My Aunt Agatha, in fact, has even gone so far as to call him my keeper. Well, what I say is: Why not? The man's a genius. From the collar upwards he stands alone. I gave up trying to run my own affairs within a week of his coming to me.'—(Carry on, Jeeves. p. 2.)

Bertie was under the impression that he had chosen Jeeves, approving the man who had been sent by an agency. But that is not what happened. Proust once remarked that, 'It is a mistake to speak of a bad choice in love, since, as soon as a choice exists, it can only be bad.' Much the same can be said about Bertie's relationship with Jeeves. He was initially impressed by the way Jeeves floated noiselessly through the doorway. He was impressed again by Jeeves's recipe for a hangover. What he failed to grasp is that it was Jeeves who chose him and that the agency had not been involved. Nor did he appreciate that Jeeves's basic policy, once in Bertie's employ, was to ensure that his employer should remain a bachelor. At the time of Jeeves's arrival Bertie was actually engaged to Florence Craye. Jeeves put an end to this in a matter of days. In understanding this and other events we need to remember, first of all, that Jeeves was a much older man with a far wider experience. Even more to the point, he knew what he wanted, as Bertie had never done, and had ruled out all possible brides in advance. That he had known some of them at Picklerod Hall is highly probable but his views went beyond the consideration of any particular candidate. Bertie was his chosen employer and marriage for Bertie was out of the question. Jeeves once described Bertie as 'as essentially one of Nature's bachelors,' which was not entirely true. In so far as Jeeves could ensure it, however, a bachelor he was and a bachelor he should remain.

While effectively restrained from marrying, at least for a number of years, Bertie Wooster was not unappreciative of his female contemporaries. He once said of himself, 'Bertram Wooster is not a man who slops readily over when speaking of the other sex. He is cool and critical. He weighs his words.' It is clear moreover that he had given the subject careful thought. Nor was he himself ruled out as unacceptable except, sometimes, on the grounds of immaturity. During the period of his actively social bachelorhood his name was linked at various times with at least a dozen girls. For purposes of scholarly research they will be listed in alphabetical rather than chronological order, as follows:–

1. *Bassett, Madeline*   Only daughter of Sir Watkyn Bassett, magistrate at Bow Street. Whereas Sir W. is as tough as they come, the fair Madeline was 'the sloppiest, mushiest, sentimentalist young Gawd-help–us who ever thought that the stars were God's daisy-chain and that every time a fairy hiccoughs a wee baby is born.' She had designs on Bertie at one time but he saw the danger, classified her as, 'The Woman Whom God Forgot', and was gratified to

hear of her marrying Roderick Spode, Lord Sidcup.*

2. *Craye, Florence* Daughter of the Earl of Worplesdon, a girl with a lovely profile and platinum blonde hair, tall, willowy and handsome, but the whole effect ruined by intellectual gifts and a serious purpose. Bertie was twice engaged to her and can be said to have had a narrow escape. At one point she made him read a book called *Types of Ethical Theory*. Her young brother was a malevolent boy scout whose purpose was (if anything) more serious still.

3. *Glossop, Honoria Jane Louise* Only daughter of Sir Roderick Glossop, the nerve specialist or alienist. She was a Girton product, 'One of those robust girls with the muscles of a welterweight and a laugh like a squadron of cavalry charging over a tin bridge', who tires you out on the golf course and then expects you take an intelligent interest in Freud. She was clever enough to realize that it was Jeeves who prevented Bertie from marrying.

4. *Mills, Phyllis* Step-daughter of the Rev. Aubrey Upjohn, (headmaster of Bertie's Prep School) an extremely pretty young prune with a face of the Souls Awakening type. She married Walter Cream.

5. *Pendlebury, Gwladys* A Chelsea artist. Relevant to her is a pregnant saying of Bertie's Aunt Dahlia, 'No good can come of association with anything labelled Gwladys or Isobel or Ethyl or Maybelle or

---

* Roderick Spode was for some years the leader of the Black Shorts movement in Britain, a movement deriving its inspiration from the Fascist movement in Italy. The movement still exists under some other name but Roderick Spode resigned the leadership when his father's death made him Lord Sidcup. Whether his views actually changed at this moment we do not know but he evidently felt that black shorts would be inappropriate in the House of Lords; a conclusion with which most people would agree.

Kathryn. But particularly Gwladys.' Bertie took heed of this warning, and very right too.

6. *Potter-Pirbright, Cora* (Corky) The film star, of shattering beauty and super-charged vitality, who was (like Aunt Agatha in this respect only) authoritative. 'When she wants you to do a thing, you find yourself doing it.' She luckily decided to marry Esmond Haddock of King's Deverill.

7. *Pringle, Heloise* Daughter of Professor Pringle. First cousin to Honoria Glossop, whom she closely resembled.

8. *Singer, Muriel* A quiet appealing girl of a dangerous type who luckily married Bruce Corcoran.

9. *Slingsby, Beatrice* Once admired by Bertie but soon safely married to Alexander Slingsby.

10. *Stoker, Pauline* Daughter of J. Washburn Stoker of East 67th St New York City. She was engaged to Bertie for 48 hours but eventually married Lord Chuffnell.

11. *Wickham, Roberta* Only daughter of the late Sir Cuthbert and Lady Wickham, of Skeldings Hall, Herts. A fiery red-haired girl of startling beauty and impudence, wooed by successive suitors and adept at playing them off against each other. She knew every hellish trick and had been a menace since childhood being (it was said) charming, unscrupulous, quarrelsome, mettlesome, quick to tears and quick to wrath. Bertie was twice engaged to her and Jeeves had the greatest difficulty in convincing him that red-haired girls are to be shunned like the devil.

12. *Wickhammersley, Cynthia* Younger daughter of the Rt. Hon. the Earl of Wickhammersley. With her Bertie was in love, although he had to admit that she was full of ideas and all that. She finally concluded that he was weak in the head, a theory which might be incorrect but was at times difficult to refute.

From even a cursory glance over this list, it must be apparent that Bertie's bachelor status was always at risk. As against that, it is manifest that he could never have married Madeline Bassett, Florence Craye, Honoria Glossop, Cora Potter-Pirbright or Heloise Pringle; nor, had there been a marriage with any of them could it have lasted a year. Of the others, one or two came near to understanding him and one, as we shall see, was to end as his quite admirable wife. In the meanwhile, our task is to gain a general idea of the way he lived and of the use which Jeeves was to make of him. More especially must we see his life from Jeeves's point of view. Bertie Wooster's career is not irrelevant to our story but it is the life of Jeeves we are trying to illustrate, follow and explain.

If Jeeves had (like Miss Jean Brodie) a Prime, it must have been during his association with Bertie Wooster. Looking back on it, moreover, he would have seen these years as divided between London, Worcestershire, and New York. We have seen already that Jeeves's London did not extend far beyond Mayfair; that Jeeves, like Bertie, was never seen in any area east of Leicester Square.

It remains, however, to define Woostershire, the part of England in which Bertie and Jeeves were more often to be seen. It lies north of Gloucester, the Worcester road passing between Totleigh Towers and Twing Hall. Far to your right, in Hertfordshire, are Woollan Chersey and Skeldings Hall. Heading still further north you have Kingham Manor, near Pershore, and, north-west of Worcester, you come to Market Snodsbury, near which is Brinkley Court. As you approach Kidderminster you have Corfly Hall on you left and Much Middleford and Easiby Hall on your right, east of which and some distance away, in Southmoltonshire, there is Rowcester Abbey. North of Kidderminster, you find

Market Blandings in Shropshire, dominated by Blandings Castle, and closely adjacent the picturesque Wooster Castle which has belonged for centuries to the Earls of Yaxley. All the area so far decribed is known, in literary circles, as Woostershire although there is no actual county of that name. We would be quite wrong, of course, to suppose that Jeeves was never outside that area. We know, for example, that his career began in Hampshire and that his biographer cannot avoid reference to Sussex, Kent, Oxfordshire and Somerset. In general, however, the Wooster country is fairly well defined and there is no question of any civilized person going further north than Leicester or Shrewsbury.

In his later reminiscences Jeeves is quite frank about his reaction to Bertie Wooster's occasional thoughts of marriage. 'I had no desire,' he writes, 'to sever a connection so pleasant in every respect as his and mine had been, and my experience is that whereas the wife comes in at the front door the valet of bachelor days goes out at the back.' The policy he pursued is one that we can understand. But his influence was not merely negative. He saved Bertie from many a disaster and extricated him from many a seemingly impossible situation. It would take volumes to describe even a tithe of these incidents, for Bertie was accident prone, wandering from one sad predicament to the next.

There was, to begin with, his engagement to the domineering Florence Craye which Jeeves knew how to terminate. Then came the awkward situation when Heloise Pringle took Bertie under her wing, remarking incidentally (as Honoria Glossop had done), 'I don't like Jeeves,' and again it was Jeeves who averted the disaster. Now in London, and often at Brinkley Hall, Twing Hall or Totleigh Towers, as the case might be, Bertie pursued his round of visits, attended nearly always by the faithful Jeeves. And the merit of this Edwardian pattern of life, from our point of view, was to give Jeeves a continually changing scene, with different scenery, different company and different gossip. In after years he would say, 'Those were the days,' and tell again the story, with advantages, of the Prize Giving at Market Snodbury Grammar School, the Great Sermon Handicap, or of how he (Jeeves) made a useful appearance as Chief Inspector Witherspoon of Scotland Yard.

Where so much is to tell and where so much has already been told it is essential to separate somehow the significant from the trivial, the significant parts being those of course which happen to interest us. In the Jeeves –Wooster Saga the significant passages relate to one or other of the two central themes; one being the character of Roberta (or Bobbie) Wickham, the other being the growth of Jeeves's practice as an adviser to all the young men about town. Of Bobbie Wickham we have read several descriptions and we should be justified in concluding that she was adorable, with auburn hair, perfect figure and tip-tilted nose, pretty hands and the sort of smile that seems to light up the whole neighbourhood. Bertie fell in love with her while staying for Christmas, on Lady Wickham's invitation, at Skeldings Hall. Jeeves promptly advised him against proposing to her, using these words, '. . . considered as a matrimonial prospect for a gentleman of your description, I cannot look upon her as suitable. In my opinion Miss Wickham lacks seriousness, sir. She is too volatile and frivolous. To qualify as Miss Wickham's husband a gentleman would need to possess a commanding personality and considerable strength of character.'

'Exactly!' said Bertie.

'I would also hesitate to commend as a life's companion a young lady with quite such a vivid shade

of red hair. Red hair, sir, in my opinion, is dangerous.'*

Bertie scorned this advice as mere rubbish (after all
her hair was auburn, surely?) and prepared to enjoy the
festive season. Having a slight grudge against Hilde-
brand (Tuppy) Glossop, nephew of Sir Roderick Glossop
and a fellow guest at Skeldings, Bertie mentioned the
fact to Bobbie. She advised him to tie a darning needle to
the end of a long stick, enter Tuppy's room late at night,
shove the needle through the bed clothes and puncture
Tuppy's hot-water bottle. This had been a merely
routine procedure at the girls' school which she had
attended. Delighted with the idea (how could that ass
Jeeves describe her as frivolous?), Bertie made the raid as
planned, unaware that there had been a change of plans
and that the bed he was to assail was that of Sir Roderick
Glossop. He was caught in the act, needless to say. Sir
Roderick, convinced in any case that Bertie was insane,
commandeered Bertie's room and left that lunatic to
make what he could of the sodden bed in which he, Sir
Roderick, had begun this eventful night. Hardly was Sir
Roderick asleep when Tuppy entered what has been
Bertie's room and punctured what he took to be Bertie's
hot-water bottle with a darning needle tied to the end of
a stick. It transpired, in fact, that Bobbie had made the
suggestion to both of them and that Jeeves, incidentally,
had been party to the double plot. Annoyed as he might
be with Jeeves, Bertie's love for Bobbie had seemingly

* Jeeves, as we have seen (pp. 23–38) had learnt in early life that red-haired
girls are a menace to society. His experiences had been peculiar and his
conclusions cannot be accepted without allowing some examples to the
contrary. One scholar has suggested that Jeeves had actually known
Roberta Wickham at Picklerod Academy but a study of the Academy's
records has shown this to be untrue. Roberta was at one time at a finishing
school in Switzerland, from which she was expelled (as must happen to
many a high-spirited girl) but saw nothing at any time of Picklerod.

died at that moment of history. (*Very Good Jeeves*, Chapter III)

While romance was a thing of the past, Bertie and Bobbie Wickham still moved in the same circle and met each other repeatedly. Lady Wickham, a woman of commanding presence, had her own plans for Bobbie whose future husband she saw as a Duke or at least as a millionaire. Lowering her sights one summer, she decided that Bobbie should marry the prosperous Mr Clifford Gandle, MP once President of the Union at Oxford and seen as a future member of the Cabinet. Lady Wickham, a novelist of some note, asked Gandle to stay at Skeldings Hall, having also invited Mr Potter, an American publisher, at the same time. Working in a mysterious way her wonders to perform, Bobbie told Mr Gandle, in strict confidence, that Mr Potter was a suicidal maniac. With the same look of transparent sincerity, she told Mr Potter that Mr Gandle was a homicidal maniac, one of a family that had been mad for generations. After a complex series of improbable incidents Lady Wickham asked a rhetorical question, 'Is everybody mad?'

To which Bobbie replied. 'I think Clifford Gandle must be. You know, these men who do wonderful things at the University often do crack up suddenly. I was reading a case only yesterday about a man in America. He took every possible prize at Harvard or wherever it was, and then, just as everybody was predicting a most splendid future for him, he bit his aunt . . .'

The idea of her marrying Mr Gandle, who had already proposed to her, was now abandoned. Encouraged by the result of this and perhaps some other episodes, Bertie would seem to have shown a renewed interest, proposing to Bobbie again, at which point she laughed like a bursting paper bag and told him not to be a silly ass. The greater, therefore, was his surprise when he saw in *The Times* that:

> The engagement is announced between Bertram Wilberforce Wooster of Crighton Mansions, W.1, and Roberta, daughter of the late Sir Cuthbert Wickham and Lady Wickham of Skeldings Hall, Herts.

It was a moment for decisive action and he drove down to Brinkley Court where Bobbie was to be found. There she was and she calmly explained that she was in love with Reggie (i.e. Kipper) Herring and that this announcement was to prepare the way for their alliance. If Lady Wickham (who detested Bertie – see page 124 above) thought that Bobbie and Bertie were engaged, only to be told that it was all a mistake, she would be so thankful that even Reggie would seem acceptable. Bertie, who would never fail to help a pal, agreed to pursue the charade for a week or two, at which point the girl said: 'I'm awfully fond of you, Bertie.'

'Me, too, of you' (he replied)

'But I can't marry everybody, can I?'

'I wouldn't even try . . .'

There was still some affection between them but Bertie realized that Bobbie was liable to produce at any moment one of those schemes which stagger humanity and turn the moon to blood, immersing some male (and, probably Bertie) in what Shakespeare calls a sea of troubles. He was daily so immersed and had to explain at one point that he himself liked a quiet life whereas, 'Roberta Wickham wouldn't recognize the quiet life if you brought it to her on a plate with watercress round it.'

Her diabolical scheme having had a measure of success, Bobbie and Reggie became engaged and it might have looked, for a while, as if all problems had been solved. In point of fact, they were not. In Reggie, a strong man with a past reputation as an amateur boxer, Bobbie had met rather more than her match. He stood up to her all too effectively. Worse was to follow when he wrote a critical review of a novel which Lady Wickham had published under a pseudonym. Roberta began to have her doubts and suspect that Reggie was a domineering type. She resented his effort to assert himself and broke off the engagement as the result of an unusually dramatic quarrel, in the course of which he called her a carrot-topped Jezebel and she called him a fat-headed nincompoop. On this note an otherwise beautiful relationship was brought to an end.

The other central theme which can be traced through the years when Jeeves and Bertie Wooster were together was, as we have seen, the growth of Jeeves's consulting practice. When extricated from any difficult situation it was Bertie's habit to reward Jeeves with a suitable sum of money. The sums thus paid were fairly small but those paid by other young men were a great deal more generous. We have all too little information about Jeeves's practice, the work being highly confidential and the results being merely rumoured, but there is reason to believe that Jeeves earned a considerable income. Nor can we doubt that he doubled it through his knowledge of the turf. At a later stage in his life Jeeves turned out to be a man of means, with money to invest. There were those (and Bertie Wooster among them) who would wonder why a man with Jeeves's brains should have been content, in the first place, with a merely domestic role in life. The fact is, however, that he was more prosperous than his friends realized and able to find enjoyment in the part he had chosen to play. In many another career he would have had rivals and might well have had to admit that some were superior to him in this, that or the other respect. As a butler he could never have been superior to Lord Emsworth's Beach, to Lord Ufferham's Keggs, or, for that matter, to his own uncle Silversmith. But in the special world of the Drones Club and the Junior Ganymede, Jeeves had gained an eminence which might, in another calling, have eluded him. In the world of gentlemen's personal gentlemen, Jeeves was one of the immortals. It could be said of him (and often was said of him) that he stood alone.

Of Bertie Wooster's relatives the most formidable, as we all know, was Aunt Agatha. She stood five foot nine in height and was topped off with a beaky nose, a lot of grey hair and the eye of a man-eating fish. To Bertie she was the aunt who ate broken bottles, killed rats with her teeth, wore barbed wire next to her skin and turned periodically into a werewolf. Jeeves was, naturally, more restrained in his references to Aunt Agatha but he did observe on one occasion, quoting Shakespeare:

> '. . . *were she other than she is,*
> *she were unhandsome; and being no*
> *other but as she is, I do not*
> *like her.*'

She was not wholly unattractive in her younger days and had been briefly engaged to the Hon. Percival Craye but the fixture was scratched when she saw in her evening newspaper that he had been thrown out of a Covent

Garden Ball and arrested in company with a girl called Tottie. Our immediate sources of reference give Lushington as the girl's surname but historians have always assumed that this must have been Margot Asquith, who was always called Tottie among her friends. Be that as it may, the engagement was broken off and Agatha married a successful stockbroker called Spencer Gregson, who acquired Woollam Chersey Manor in Hertfordshire.

Gregson she remained for much of her life and presented an ungrateful world with her son, Thomas, who combined his mother's ruthlessness with his father's commercial genius. Brought up with Thomas was Augustus Wooster, the only son of the late Henry Wooster, who had ended in a mental home. Gussie, who was of course Bertie's cousin, was a complete contrast to Thomas, a rather subdued character who seldom spoke except to say 'Very well, Aunt Agatha.' As for the Hon. Percival Craye, who became the Rt. Hon. the Earl of Worplesdon (see pp. 39–40) he also married and had two children, Lady Florence Craye (see p. 119) to whom Bertie was once briefly engaged, and Edwin, the boy scout, wisely avoided by everyone. The Earl was left a widower and, thirty years after the original engagement, married Agatha Spencer Gregson, now also widowed. They lived thereafter at his residence, Steeple Bumpleigh Hall in Hampshire.

If Aunt Agatha had been overbearing before, a fact beyond dispute, she was doubly so as from the day when she became Countess of Worplesdon. She was, as Bertie remarked, 'a well bred vulture', and all in her vicinity jumped to do her bidding. But even she came to recognize that she had overdone the reign of terror where her nephew Gussie was concerned. Spiritless from childhood, he had been sent to Malvern House preparatory school where he had been, like Bertie, a pupil of the Rev. Aubrey Upjohn. Still further crushed at that hellish establishment, he went to one of the smaller public schools and so to Oxford. What career he was to follow was much in doubt and he himself expressed no preference of any kind. Faced with this listless character, the Earl of Worplesdon applied the only remedy which would occur to the Chairman and principal shareholder of the Pink Funnel Line. The boy should go to sea as assistant purser and the experience would make a man of him. Whether his successive voyages in the *Pinkgin* had so dramatic an effect on him we hardly know but they did remove him from the immediate vicinity of Aunt Agatha.

For a year or so he moved back and forth between Southampton and Montevideo and then his ship was ordered to New York which was for her an unusual port of call. From there the Earl received two cables, one from his agents to say that Gussie had quitted his appointment and gone ashore, the other (some weeks later) from Gussie, to say that he proposed to marry a Vaudeville actress called Jacqueline Fitzroy. It would seem that years of repression had at last produced a feeble attempt at mutiny.

Aunt Agatha's reaction was circumspect. At her instigation the Earl of Worplesdon summoned Bertie Wooster to have lunch with him at the Carlton Club. He was to make it clear that Bertie was to cross the Atlantic, find young Gussie and persuade him to think again. But why should Bertie be the chosen envoy? The question which the reader may ask was the question asked by Bertie himself and might well have occurred to anyone else. The answer, however, is simple. Everyone else had refused, except indeed those considered unsuitable in the first place. No good advice would reach Gussie from the mouths of Uncle Willoughby or old Sir George, no good influence would come from Claude or Eustace.

Bertie was the man available and the one who could be bullied into it. But was he the man to handle a delicate situation with finesse? No one could suppose that he was, but Jeeves would be with him and it was on his brains that Aunt Agatha had learnt to rely. In Germany of the Hohenzollerns it was the custom to appoint a Chief of Staff to direct a campaign and then remember, as an afterthought, to appoint a Commander-in-Chief. In some such fashion young Gussie's relatives sent Jeeves to the rescue but with Bertie in nominal command. They could see that the situation was a difficult one but they looked upon Jeeves as their trump card. He, if anyone, would know exactly what to do.

'So you see what the situation is,' concluded Worplesdon, 'It is a case, you may think, of a young man being almost over-disciplined and over-protected in childhood.'

'You may say that again!' Bertie replied.

'Of course I shall say it again if I want to,' replied the short-tempered Earl. 'And what I mean to say is that young Gussie has too little initiative, too little knowledge of the world. He falls for the first woman who gives him the least encouragement.'

'And what is known about her?'

'Well, Jacqueline Fitzroy is obviously an unusual name.'

'Yes, yes, of course.'

'And she appears in Vaudeville.* That is a type of stage entertainment in which short acts succeed each

---

* Vaudeville. Les Vaux de Vire were originally songs attributed to Olivier Basselin. The term was applied to American variety entertainment of a type popular from about 1880 to 1932. The merit of this type of show lay in the fact that the convivial patron could arrive or go at any time, secure in the knowledge that what he saw would be wholly unrelated to previous and subsequent scenes. A musical comedy, by contrast, is supposed to have a plot.

other, slapstick turns, song and dance routines, juggling performers and impersonations.'

'Just so,' replied Bertie, who knew about Vaudeville. 'And what part does she perform?'

'She assists the conjurer, handing him his hat and disposing of the rabbits. I see her as doing this in the minimum of clothing.'

'I can imagine,' said Bertie, whose imagination was fully equal to the task.

'Such a woman would be a most unsuitable wife for your Aunt Agatha's nephew. So your mission will be to break it up, explaining to Gussie that he should marry into a county family and that he should come home at once.'

'I get the idea. Has Gussie any money?'

'Not from me, not after that second cable.'

'Do you have his address in New York?'

'No, we don't. You will have to find him. Your aunt will pay your expenses – your reasonable expenses, I should say. Cabin class or thereabouts – no luxury suite opening on the promenade deck. She assumes, moreover, that Jeeves will travel with you and that you will not be without his advice.'

'I don't know where she gets the idea that Jeeves is so essential. Still, it's true that I wouldn't go without him. Very well then. I'll do it, sailing within a few days. I'll cable you when I have located Gussie and then cable you the date of his return. I don't fancy that I shall have any difficulty. I have often thought that I should be a diplomatist or perhaps a secret agent.'

'A diplomatist? You? Ah, well, you now have the chance to prove how successful you would have been.' The Earl shuddered at this thought but went on bravely, 'And New York may well be worth a visit – Carnegie Falls, the Statute of Liberty and all that sort of thing.' The lunch ended on an amicable note and Bertie soon found himself on board the *Gastromania*, the family's chosen agent on a difficult mission.

Bertie stayed briefly at the Algonquin but moved soon afterwards to a flat in East 57th Street. It was Jeeves who found the flat but it was the last service he was to perform for some weeks. It will or will not be recalled that an absent-minded friend of Wooster's called Biffen had married a girl called Mabel who turned out to be Jeeves's niece. They had met during a transatlantic passage while Mr Biffen, owner of an estate in Herefordshire, was on his way to do some salmon fishing in Canada. Some time after the marriage he resolved to resume his campaign against the Canadian salmon but this time with an attractive wife to encourage him. There now arrived from Mrs Biffen an appeal to Jeeves by telegram. Her husband was missing and she did not know what to do about it. With anyone else the fear might well have been that a salmon had bitten him or that he had been drowned or at least seriously injured after going over Niagara Falls. But old Biffy was a peculiar case. The likelihood with him was that he had lost his way and then forgotten the name of the place at which he was staying. The difficulties would not be insuperable but it was clear that Mabel needed her uncle's help.

Kind-hearted as ever, Bertie was more than willing to spare Jeeves and perhaps the more so in that he now had the chance to show what he could accomplish on his own. Nor were his efforts initially misdirected. He discovered that the Vaudeville shows on Broadway numbered five. Of these two had no conjurer, having performing animals instead. Obtaining programmes for the other three, he quickly ascertained that Jacqueline Fitzroy played her humble role at the Alhambra Palace in West 48th Street. It could not be said that her name was in lights but it was there in the programme. With an almost Napoleonic sense of strategy, Bertie decided to watch the stage door, feeling certain that Gussie must appear there before long. His patience was soon rewarded and he quickly hailed Gussie as a friend, explaining that he just happened to be passing and that it was (and is) a small world, what!

It cannot be said that Gussie was unduly cordial on this occasion – he seemed to have something else on his mind – but he reluctantly gave Bertie his telephone number and agreed to lunch with him two days hence at Sardi's East. Over that lunch Gussie spoke of Jacqueline at length – her beauty, her talent, her brains and her modesty. She was, he explained, a girl in a million. 'That being so,' said Bertie with great cunning, 'she would do better in Hollywood.'

'But I can't part with her, and my job here is as a Clerk in the Head Office of the Bright Star Shipping Line.'

'But, surely, Gussie, aren't you being a little selfish? Should you be the one to stand in the way of her career? And won't her success make it easier for your aunt and uncle to accept her as one of the family?'

Gussie was unconvinced but Bertie knew what to do next. Going to Finkelbaum and Grabstein, the theatrical agents, Bertie asked whether if it would be possible to arrange a screen test in Hollywood for a gifted actress, presently well known on Broadway.

'Maybe it could, maybe it couldn't, replied Mr Finkelbaum (or possibly Mr Grabstein) 'Whasser name?'

'Jacqueline Fitzroy, currently playing at the Alhambra Palace.'

'That crumby joint. Playing the lead, you said?'

'Well – playing a strong supporting role.'

'Who'll pay her fare to L.A.?'

'I will.'

'And a commission to me?'

'Sure.' (Bertie was learning the language)

'It would be a test with the Perfecto Zizzbaum Motion Picture Corporation. Mr Schnellenhamer happens to be a pal of mine. Yessir. I can fix it. And let's hope the little lady lands a contract, with me of course as her agent. How's that for service, eh, Mr Booster?'

All was arranged and Bertie, after a week or two, asked Gussie to dine with him at the Barbizon Plaza. The moment had come to talk Gussie into the idea of booking his passage to Southampton. But Gussie appeared in a rather belligerent mood. Waving a newspaper, he asked Bertie whether he had seen the latest news about Jacqueline? Bertie shook his head and read the paragraphs to which Gussie pointed with a shaking finger. From all points of view they could not have been less welcome or more disturbing.

CONTRACT AT FIRST SIGHT

Mr Levitsky of Perfecto Zizzbaum has the name of a man who looks before he leaps, but he wasted no time when he saw the screen test of Miss Jacqueline Fitzroy, actress from Broadway, but signed her on for his new motion picture *Little Lord Fauntleroy*.* With her exceptional beauty and outstanding talent, her face, English accent and distinguished poise she is perfect for the part. Mr Levitsky always maintains that Zizzbaum is not Perfecto for nothing. In his productions everything must be authentic and all he needs now for this new picture is the perfect English butler, more difficult to find, he says, than an authentically aristocratic English lady. Although a newcomer to Hollywood Miss Fitzroy has already attracted a great deal of attention and was recently seen at Romanov's with no less a squire than Roger Standish, whose fifth and current wife Norma

---

* *Little Lord Fauntleroy*. This particular version of that nauseating book was never shown on the screen and is not to be confused with other versions to which the public has since been exposed.

Gladwell was there the same evening with Don Devlin, the star of *Dawn on the Desert*. The scene might have been embarrassing but she took it in good part and the more so in that it was Norma's birthday.

Readers of motion picture gossip are apt to suspect that stage names are all fictitious and we were ourselves inclined to think that Miss Fitzroy's real name might be something less distinguished like Huggins or Batty. However, our gossip columnist, Rita Pryall, made a transatlantic call to the present Duchess of Grafton, whose husband is head of the Fitzroy family, and asked her whether Jacqueline is a relative. She laughed, explaining that Jacqueline is indeed the Duke's first cousin and therefore a direct descendant of King Charles II. She was amused to hear of Jacqueline's latest escapade and remarked that she had been a debutante three seasons ago. Rita asked the Duchess whether she would regard the wealthy Roger Standish as a suitable husband for her young relative. 'I doubt,' replied the Duchess, 'whether young Jacqueline would care to be anyone's sixth wife. She is a considerable heiress you know, on her mother's side.'

Alongside these paragraphs was a picture of Jacqueline, looking perfectly lovely and almost incredibly innocent.

'Ah!' said Bertie, and added, 'Oh!' for good measure. We should not go too far if we were to say that he was taken aback. He could not imagine what this stunning girl could see in Gussie but he could readily understand that Gussie would want to bring her back from Hollywood. Had he to fetch her in a covered waggon pursued by Red Indians he would have set off that evening without hesitation, clutching his shotgun and prepared to leave a trail of corpses across the prairie. In point of fact, the problem was less daunting than that but a great deal more complex. It would involve the breaking of a contract with Perfecto Zizzbaum, no laughing matter at any time. At this moment in the drama Gussie did not know that Bertie was responsible for the disaster. It was Aunt Agatha who knew of his machinations (reported by mail) and who now realized how unfortunate his intervention had been. So the two young men dined together amicably and Bertie braced himself to face the storm which would break, as he guessed, on the following day. It came in the form of a cable from Aunt Agatha, one concluded in terms which were as unfair as they were unmerited, as eloquent as they were rude.

NO ONE IN THE WORLD BUT YOU (IT BEGAN) COULD HAVE MADE SO COMPLETE A MESS OF SO SIMPLE AN ERRAND STOP GUSSIE COULD NOT HAVE FOUND NO MORE SUITABLE BRIDE THAN JACQUELINE FITZROY STOP WHY HAD YOU TO INTERFERE SO STUPIDLY BEFORE YOU HAD EVEN SEEN THE GIRL QUERY STOP TRY TO UNDO THE DAMAGE YOU HAVE DONE BUT NOT WITHOUT THE ADVICE OF JEEVES STOP TRY NOT TO BE AS IDIOTIC AGAIN AND AVOID GOING BEYOND WHAT YOU HAVE BEEN ASKED TO DO STOP IF YOU HAVE RUINED GUSSIE'S LIFE AS SEEMS PROBABLE YOU WILL NEVER BE FORGIVEN BY YOUR AUNT AGATHA WORPLESDON.

This cable was enough to spoil any chap's appetite for lunch but there is a providence which protects the nitwits of the world and Bertie was a little consoled by receiving, later that day, a telegram which read as follows:

MISSION ACCOMPLISHED AM RETURNING P.M. TOMORROW — JEEVES.

Jeeves's actual return made Bertie feel a new man but he was polite enough to ask first for news of the Biffens.

'Well, sir,' said Jeeves, 'the position was very much as I had anticipated. Mr Biffen was hopelessly lost and had forgotten the name of his hotel and the name of the place in which that hotel is situated.'

'He remembered his own name?'

'Yes, sir.'

'And he remembered that he has a wife?'

'Yes, sir.'

'But the mind was otherwise blank?'

'It would seem so, Mr Wooster.'

'So what did you do?'

'I made contact, sir, with the Canadian Mounted Police.'

'Who always get their man?'

'Eventually, sir. Mr Biffen was located yesterday and is now restored to his anxious wife.'

'But it's all a bit worrying, eh? He may get lost again at any time, after all.'

'No, sir. I have now provided against that. Mr Biffen has a monomark and certain telephone numbers tattooed on his posterior.'

'Well done, Jeeves. A smart idea, but why on his bottom?'

'Because it won't show, sir, when Mr Biffen goes swimming. And may I ask whether you yourself, sir, have had any crisis in my absence?'

'Have I—? You will never know, Jeeves, what I have been through. I'll try, all the same, to give you the gist of it, the bare outline. You remember the problem about Mr Augustus Wooster?'

'Yes, sir.'

'Well, it all began when I traced this girl to the Alhambra Palace . . .' Bertie concluded his story by showing Jeeves the newspaper references to Jacqueline and, finally, the cable received yesterday from Aunt Agatha. 'This time, Jeeves,' he concluded, 'I'm in real trouble.'

'Most disturbing, sir.'

'I can't describe the agonies I suffer.'

'No, sir? Shakespeare once put it rather well in *Henry VI*, Part III:

> *"Our hap is loss, our hope but sad despair;*
> *Our ranks are broke, and ruin follows us:*
> *What counsel give you? whither shall we fly?"'*

'Shakespeare wrote that, did he?'

'Yes, sir. In Act II, Scene IV.'

'He must have had at least one aunt. But what am I to do?'

'The problem requires careful thought, sir.'

'You bet it does. So think, Jeeves, as never before!'

'Yes, sir. My conclusion is that I had better travel to Los Angeles and persuade Mr Levitsky to cancel his contract with Miss Fitzroy.'

'But he won't be such an ass, Jeeves. A producer who has that girl under contract will cling to her like glue.'

'Perhaps, sir, we should study the contract. I should suppose that the theatrical agents will have a copy.'

'Brilliant, Jeeves – so they will!'

And so indeed they had. Within the hour Jeeves had the contract before him in Messrs Finkelbaum and Grabstein's office.

'An interesting document,' he said at last. 'Very precise about what she is to do and what she is to be paid. Not so detailed, sir, about what she is to refrain from doing.'

'What do you mean, Jeeves? I don't get the idea.'

'Well, sir, she has to be at the studio as directed and perform her part to the best of her ability. There is no clause to prevent her calling Mr Levitsky a cheap skate whenever she sees him.'

'True, Jeeves. She might even call him a slob.'

'That might well be the term she would prefer to use,

sir. Nor is it anywhere stated that she must not throw things at him.'

'Nor it is, Jeeves. Potatoes, for example. Any high spirited girl might carry a bagful for that very purpose.'

'Or tomatoes, sir, as her mood might suggest.'

'But, look, Jeeves, I suppose these contracts must be all the same. Why don't other players pelt Levitsky and Schellenhamer with rotten eggs?'

'Other players, sir, hope to be employed again in that or some other studio. Miss Fitzroy, I should assume, has no such long-term ambitions.'

'Can we be sure of that, Jeeves?'

'I think, sir, we can be reasonably confident. Work in motion pictures is not attractive in itself. Players are expected to be in the studio at an unusually early hour and the work is tedious in itself. Even the most dedicated actor is apt to lose interest after the thirty-second re-take of the same sequence in which the same character falls over the same bucket of whitewash. My guess would be sir, that Miss Fitzroy has already had more than enough.'

Bertie was at first inclined to go in person to Hollywood but Jeeves dissuaded him, arguing that he would do better to stay in New York and write soothing letters to his aunt. In the end Jeeves made the journey alone and made contact with Miss Fitzroy at the Hollywood Knickerbocker Hotel.* He had been quite right to assume that she was already bored with motion pictures but she was too nice a girl to use the language

* The Hollywood Knickerbocker Hotel was at this time the known resort of people with fringe functions on the outskirts of the Motion Picture Industry. Agents and go-betweens would congregate there in order to tell each other that such-and-such a property would make a great, indeed a stupendous film. Few if any of these characters had either money or influence and the general atmosphere could not but help a girl to decide against Hollywood altogether.

suggested. She was willing and eager to throw tomatoes but her aim was deplorable and Mr Levitsky was practically the only person on the set to remain unscathed. Over her contract it was finally necessary to compromise and Bertie received the following telegram:

TOMATOES OFF TARGET BUT LEVITSKY FINALLY AGREED TO CANCEL CONTRACT ON CONDITION THAT I PLAY THE ROLE OF BUTLER IN FILM STOP SHOOTING TIME SHOULD BE APPROXIMATELY THREE WEEKS STOP MISS FITZROY RETURNING AT ONCE TO NEW YORK STOP SUGGEST THAT MR AUGUSTUS WOOSTER MEET THE TRAIN FROM LOS ANGELES AT 2015 THIS WEDNESDAY JEEVES.

All Jeeves's arrangements went according to plan and Gussie met Jacqueline with an armful of flowers and a repeated and urgent proposal, which was not, however, immediately accepted. As for Bertie Wooster he was left again without Jeeves and even attempted, on occasion, to make his own early morning tea. To his letters addressed to the Countess of Worplesdon he received no reply and he accordingly decided to stay in New York for a further period of months, having made many friends and having learnt his way round the local amenities. While the situation remained as it was he decided that there was no room in London for himself and Aunt Agatha. There was a clear choice, the metropolis could have one or the other but not both.

After Gussie and Jacqueline sailed for Britain, he settled down to the social life he preferred. One of his friends was Ed Pollock, who one day gave a dinner party at the Starlight Roof. The mixed party numbered about twenty and Bertie had been included so as to balance the numbers, Ed having with him an unmarried sister. Conspicuous among the guests was Mr J. Washburn Stoker, who was accompanied by his daughter Pauline. By a little inquiry Bertie established the fact that J.W.S. was a millionaire who lived at an address in East 67th Street, came originally from Carterville, Kentucky and had made a fortune from bootlegging in the good old days. He was also the presumed heir to his second cousin, George Stoker, an even wealthier man but one whose sanity was said to be in doubt. There are poor millionaires and rich millionaires, J.W. being in the former, George in the latter category. Bertie took some of this in but paid closer attention to Pauline, a girl of really startling beauty. She was a brunette with long straight hair, attractive figure, perfect oval face and happy expression. Feeling at the time just a little jealous of his cousin Gussie (because Jacqueline, after all, had been something rather special) Bertie moved in with commendable speed and asked her to join him and others in a picnic next day on Long Island. She accepted as they danced together and it seemed to Bertie that his self promotion scheme was going rather well. He did nothing to conceal his adoration and she seemed to respond with a friendliness which she did not bestow on everyone. Looking over the lights of New York below them it seemed quite natural that they should be holding hands, and when it came to saying goodbye it seemed quite inevitable that they should kiss. Nor did it seem to Bertie that Mr J. Washburn Stoker looked on their friendship with disapproval. The old pirate had a massive figure and a penetrating glance, looking as if many a victim had walked his plank, but he said good night to Bertie with something well short of actual hostility.

The picnic on the beach at Long Island was a great success. The party numbered eight, four of either sex, and it seemed generally accepted that Pauline belonged to Bertie. They held hands again and she said that his English accent was cute. When she said, 'C'mon and swim!' he responded with enthusiasm, thinking that it might end with a romp in the shallows. It actually ended in a fast swim of something over a mile. He came in a bad second and somewhat exhausted, only to find that she had brought with her a volley ball, with which they played vigorously for about an hour. Her athletic figure was now fully explained, as also perhaps the fact that other suitors had dropped for the moment out of the running. They ended that evening at a night-club and without the rest of the party. It was daylight when he saw her back to East 67th Street and there, on the sidewalk, he asked Pauline to marry him.

'I sure will!' she cooed happily, 'Come for me at eleven and we'll walk in Central Park!' She had made Bertie, as he told her, the happiest man in New York City.

After all that night-clubbing he would ordinarily have slept until midday but to-day, it seemed was to be different. After lunch she took him to a club where there were squash courts as well as a swimming pool and that evening there was a party at a friend's penthouse, with dancing again until daybreak. The Woosters are a brave family and it is known that the Sieur de Wocester fought with distinction at the Battle of Agincourt. We have to remember, however, that it was not a battle which went on for day after day. Bertie's ancestor could take it easy a bit at nightfall. His descendant, by contrast, was up against more of a marathon performance and he fairly gave up on the third day. It was all too much and he had to confess as much over the telephone. To be more precise he pleaded that he had a bad cold and must avoid passing the infection to her.

When the engaged couple met again, two days later, Pauline looked so solemn that Bertie wondered for a moment whether she too had suffered from exhaustion. He was soon undeceived on that score but she told him, nevertheless, that there were dark clouds coming over the horizon.

'You know, dearest, that my Pa is related to George Stoker, the multi-millionaire?'

'Yes, Pauline darling, that much I know.'

'Well, darling, George is such a mental case that Pa sent for a specialist from London – Sir Roderick Glossop of Harley Street. It seems that Sir Roderick knows you, Bertie.'

'He should do, darling. I was once engaged to his frightful daughter, Honoria.'

'You were? Well, we could forget about that. The trouble is that he has told my Pa that you are, in his opinion, a lunatic.'

'What absolute drivel!'

'He says that you keep twenty-three cats in your bedroom.'

'Complete rubbish!'

'Rubbish or not, Pa believes him and thinks you a poor bet as a son-in-law. I've tried to talk him round but he keeps muttering, "twenty-three!" and I can't make him see reason.'

They parted sadly that day and their engagement was ended soon afterwards by a letter from Pauline which was worded as follows:

My dear Bertie – I cannot convince Pa that you are sane. He merely reminds me that Sir Roderick is a world authority and ought to know. So he forbids our engagement and I have no alternative but must break it off and wish you better luck with another girl when Sir Roderick is somewhere else. Our days together were great fun and I shall always think of you with a sisterly affection. We had best see no more of each other for the time being but I hope we shall some day meet again as friends.

With every good wish and a final kiss
from Pauline

It is a sad moment for any of us when a lovely girl tells us that she sees our future relationship to be that of brother and sister. Bertie sighed deeply and applied a handkerchief to wipe away the expected tear. No tears came and the handkerchief remained absolutely dry. After examining the handkerchief and after a careful analysis of his feelings, Bertie came to the reluctant conclusion that he was secretly relieved. Pauline's vitality was simply too much for him. His ancestor the Sieur de Wocester might have been able to stand the pace (although Bertie was not really convinced about that) but he himself had been simply out of his league, and no kidding. He would always think of Pauline with affection but his memories would include those of being footsore, tottering and exhausted. He did not expect to recover for some days nor to feel himself again until after Jeeves had returned, which he did a few days later.

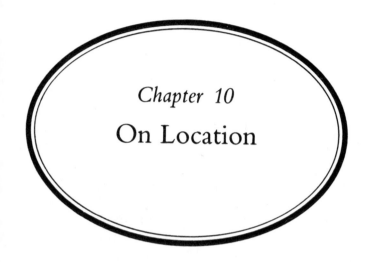

Chapter 10

On Location

Bertie Wooster's stay in New York, which was prolonged until after Gussie and Jacqueline had been safely married and Aunt Agatha to that extent appeased, had at least one unfortunate result. Bertie had taken to playing the banjolele, an instrument in current vogue which resulted, it was said, from a misalliance between a ukulele and a banjo. He was not entirely unmusical, having at one time been a choirboy and the winner, indeed, of the choirboys bicycle race, but his efforts to play his chosen instrument were unwelcome to his more immediate neighbours at Crighton Mansions, Berkeley St., W1. His renderings of various contemporary songs were the subject, in fact, of bitter complaint from, among other people, Sir Roderick Glossop, one of whose patients lived on the floor below. Another who suffered, and at closer range, was Jeeves, for whom the final straw may well have been Bertie's rendering of *Singing in the Rain*. When Bertie decided to leave town and resume his playing in some old-world country cottage, Jeeves decided to give notice. To this Bertie responded with a misquotation from the *Merchant of Venice:*

> 'The man that hath no music in himself,
> Nor is not mov'd with discord of sweet sounds
> Is fit for selling stereos at Foyle's . . .'

'I think, sir,' said Jeeves, 'that the bard wrote "Is fit for treasons, stratagems and spoils", I must insist, nevertheless, on giving you my notice.'

There was thus a clear choice before B.W. He could have the banjolele or he could have Jeeves. In no way could he have both. He chose the banjolele and Jeeves was promptly offered the post of butler to Bertie's friend, Lord Chuffnell. As successor to Jeeves, Bertie engaged a character called Brinkley, who proved anything but satisfactory. Bertie's country cottage turned out to be on Lord Chuffnell's estate but not within earshot of the Hall. So Bertie and Jeeves, going their separate ways, were still at least neighbours.

It is a solemn moment in a manservant's life when he ceases to be a valet and takes upon himself the role of butler. For Jeeves there was no mystery in the butler's art. He knew how dinner should be announced and he knew how port should be sieved. He knew, for that matter, how to stand with an expressionless face with his back against the sideboard. But the butler lives a different life from a valet, being a key figure in an established household and one in which the Master is likely to be married. In becoming a butler the former valet admits to himself that middle age has arrived. His days of roving the world as a bachelor's personal attendant are over. He is about to settle down and put on weight. What seems strange, in retrospect, is that Jeeves – so worldly wise as counsellor to Bertie – should have accepted service with the fifth baron Chuffnell. Nothing could be said against his lordship's character (although his name was Marmaduke) but he was known to be all but penniless. He lived as a bachelor at his ancestral hall, Chuffnell Hall, Chuffnell Regis, in Somerset, a building he lacked the means to maintain. Luckily for Lord Chuffnell there now appeared on the scene, by a really remarkable coincidence, Mr J. Washburn Stoker and Miss Pauline Stoker from the USA accompanied by Sir Roderick Glossop. Since Bertie's previous encounters with the Stokers, Cousin George had died, shifting J. Washburn into the multi-millionaire class, and it was now the plan that he should acquire Chuffnell Hall and restore it to use as a mental home under Sir Roderick's direction. As for Lord Chuffnell he had fallen in love with Pauline Stoker and was, luckily, her equal in outdoor activity. Events were complicated for a time – too much so for analysis – but the final upshot was fortunate for most people concerned. The fifth baron succeeded in marrying Pauline, as also in selling his ancestral home, but had to part with Jeeves, whose preference was still for bachelors and who returned to Bertie when assured that the banjolele had been burnt in a fire at the cottage.

This first rift between Bertie and Jeeves was not of long duration but their subsequent time together was to be almost as short. It is the sad fact that they were drifting apart and acquiring other interests. But here again history was to repeat itself, for Jeeves made the same mistake once more, accepting the situation of butler to William Egerton Bamfylde Ossingham Belfry, 9th Earl of Rowcester (pronounced 'Roaster') and the owner of Rowcester Abbey in Southmoltonshire. The 9th Earl was as impoverished as the fifth baron had been but with this difference that, whereas Chuffnell Hall was a merely decrepit mansion, Rowcester Abbey was little more than a picturesque ruin subject to regular flooding, a venerable structure of which only a few rooms were even habitable. To make matters worse, the Earl, though good-looking, amiable and popular, was no mental giant. His friends at the Drones Club placed him, intellectually, somewhere between Freddie Widgeon and Pongo Twiseleton, and some even guessed that his IQ was lower than that of Barmy Fotheringay-Phipps. He had found an extremely pretty girl friend in Jill Wyvern, once a dashing outside-right on the hockey field and now the local veterinary surgeon, but her earnings probably exceeded his rent roll. The Earl's prospects were very poor indeed and Jeeves soon realized that his wages were not going to be paid with regularity and might not, perhaps, be paid at all. Musing on the situation Jeeves said to himself:

> *This is the state of man: today he puts forth*
> *The tender leaves of hope; tomorrow blossoms,*
> *And bears his blushing honours thick upon him;*
> *The third day comes a frost, a killing frost,*
> *And – when he thinks, good easy man, full surely*
> *His greatness is a-ripening – nips his root,*
> (Henry the Eighth, Act III Scene II)

But Jeeves's reputation was well known and the Earl had counted on Jeeves being able to advise him. How was he to make some money? Which way should he turn? What was he to do?

When the question was fairly put to him, Jeeves replied that he himself had made money in Hollywood at the Perfecto Zizzbaum Studio. He had played the part of a butler. Perhaps there might be some other motion picture in which his lordship might play an Earl?

'And come back to find Miss Wyvern married to someone else? No, Jeeves, any filming I do must be done here.'

'That being so, I suggest that Rowcester Abbey might itself be filmed as background to a story. I venture to suggest that this might be profitable to your lordship.'

'But, look at the place, Jeeves! We have a ruined chapel and cloister, a haunted well, the remains of a tower and an overgrown churchyard. Of the actual rooms only a very few are fit to be seen, let alone filmed.'

'In Hollywood, my Lord, the indoor sequences are always shot in the studio. It is only the outdoor scenes that are shot on location. There might be a story for which this background would be ideal.'

'What sort of a story, for heaven's sake? What can you make of ruins?'

'They are not without dramatic possibilities, my lord, when seen by moonlight. When I was doing film work in a Perfecto Zizzbaum production there was talk, I remember, of a coming motion picture to be called *The Vampire of Vitriola*.'

'Good grief! A story about werewolves?'

'I fancy, my lord, that werewolves were to play some part in it. It was to be, if you follow me, a horror film. It could well be that the project has been abandoned, as happens not infrequently in Hollywood, but I could write to Mr Levitsky and enclose some camera shots of the ruined chapel. This would enable him to see the possibilities for himself:

> *"Now it is the time of night,*
> *That the graves, all gaping wide,*
> *Everyone lets forth his sprite,*
> *In the church way paths to glide."*

(Shakespeare)

Having taken in the atmosphere he might well be disposed to make your lordship an offer.'

'What – to buy the place?'

'No, my lord: merely to rent it for a period while the outside sequences were being shot; a period of weeks or possibly months. In addition to the rent, your lordship might be given a speaking part with some additional salary. There might be other and not inconsiderable sources of profit.'

'Jeeves, you are a genius!'

'I endeavour to give satisfaction, my lord.'

The odds were loaded against the success of any such scheme but the Earl was actually in luck. The 'Vampire' project was still under active consideration and this offer of a suitable location came at the right moment. Nor was it an offer to brush aside. Considered as a place to spend the night, the rat-infested Rowcester ruins could not be given high marks. As a romantic rendezvous for a honeymoon couple they would be nobody's first choice. As a place for a picnic they would be rejected at once. Looked at, however, from a different angle, any ghost would see their possibilities, any witch's coven might give them preference and any vampire would willingly pay the rent in advance. When the occasion calls for gothic windows against the darkening sky, owls hooting in the distance and nasty things being glimpsed in the tangled undergrowth, Rowcester is in a class by itself with no real competition nearer than Wales. So the cables were sent back and forth, the first payments were made, the options were agreed, the contracts were signed and the date fixed for the camera crew's arrival. At conferences held in the Perfecto Zizzbaum Head Office all were agreed that *The Vampire of Vitriola* was going to be terrifying, horrendous and terrific. With Horace Snarloff as the vampire, with Mark Fable as the hero, with Linda Pagan as the victim and Susan Hayworth as the heroine, there could be no question of failure. Beyond all possibility of doubt, beyond all argument or question, this was to be the very greatest picture of its kind.

For a frenzied period of five weeks the vicinity of Rowcester was transformed into an outdoor film set with the entire rural population required for crowd scenes. The Earl had been anxious, initially, about lack of accommodation at the Abbey. He need not have worried. Of all the people involved, whether administrative, technical or thespian, no single individual would have accepted any inducement to stay at Rowcester for the night. They all agreed that it was (a) shabby, (b) rat-infested, (c) damp, and (d) haunted. The nearest accommodation that anyone would accept was at the Dragonara Hotel, Bristol, some thirty miles away. Those most emphatic about drawback (d) were so far from wanting to spend the evening at Rowcester that they were impatient to leave at the first symptoms of approaching twilight. In point of fact, therefore, the moonlit sequences were all shot in broad daylight by cameras equipped with a darkened lens. As Jeeves had predicted, the Earl was offered a speaking part (proposing the loyal toast) while he himself was the inevitable butler and Jill Wyvern looked after the horses.

The plot involved an otherwise normal and fox-hunting family which had an undesirable ancestor still surviving in an attic and turning into a vampire with each new moon; a circumstance which was bound to lessen the value of the property and discourage young men who might otherwise have wanted to marry into the family. That was merely the basic theme. The story also involved incidental witchcraft and ghostly apparitions, enough of each to ensure that all film goers would have good value for their money. What with rent, salary, horse hire and incidental repair to some of the buildings, the Earl did very well for himself and Jeeves was thanked daily for the help he had given to the estate as well as to Perfecto Zizzbaum. He was very much the hero of the hour.

The actual director of the film was Siegfried Sevenoaks* whose temperamental changes of mind added perhaps two weeks to the time spent on location. To him neither plot nor dialogue was sacred, no scene as planned being quite ghoulish enough. For Jeeves he had a special affection because here was a man who wrote his own script as he went along. In the shooting script as issued the butler, Harkness, said little more than 'Yes, sir' and 'No, sir', but Jeeves did better than that and in phraseology beyond any ordinary script writers capacity. In the sequence, for example, which introduces Lord Mottram, a weekend guest who will wish in the end that he had not come, the butler is made to say, 'You will be in the Tower Room, Lord Mottram,' adding, to the page boy, 'Take the luggage upstairs.'

Without any conscious effort, Jeeves put this differently: 'Welcome to Vitriola, Lord Mottram. Allow me to say how pleasurable it is to see you here again. Your lordship will be in the Tower Room on this occasion. When ready, your lordship will find the other guests on the terrace. Do please ring for anything you require. (aside) Take his lordship's valise and suitcase to the Tower Room, Huggins (To Mottram again) Your servants ever have theirs, themselves, and what is theirs, in compt to make their audit at your highness' pleasure. Shakespeare. This way, my lord.'

'Cut!' shouted Siegfried. 'What's all that stuff?'

'From *Macbeth*, sir. It seemed to me that the quotation

---

* Siegfried Sevenoaks, who came from Vienna, was a well-known film director for some years but fell victim to an odd misunderstanding. He entered the cage of a gorilla whom he believed to be an actor in costume. It was the wrong cage. So ended what had seemed to be a promising career.

might seem appropriate. It was the prelude sir, in Shakespeare's play, to murder.'

'Suffering chorus girls!' groaned Siegfried, 'Would a butler quote Shakespeare?'

'I *am* a butler,' said Jeeves and Siegfried ended by letting him have his own way. Harkness was beginning to become a character in the story.

The day came when Mr Sevenoaks took Jeeves on one side and fairly told him that a film career was his for the asking. 'At Perfecto Zizzbaum we are nearly always shooting a film in which a butler is needed. Why not you? It won't make you a star – I don't pretend that it will – but you can still be on the set when half the stars have ended their career with a nervous breakdown.'

That Jeeves was tempted is certain, and indeed he was to admit as much, but he finally said 'No'.

Following the Hollywood path he might have ended with a butler of his own. What made him decide against it? We may guess, first of all, that he preferred to work for gentlemen, and that people like Schnellenhamer and Levitsky did not (in his opinion) qualify. Apart from that, however, his keenest pleasure was in solving problems for people whose ability fell short of his. People like Mr Schnellenhamer, surrounded by 'yes' men and nodders, expected more admiration than they were prepared to offer. There was no place in the Perfecto Zizzbaum Corporation for someone who would always know a better solution to every problem. Jeeves must have known this instinctively but he was profuse in his thanks for the opportunity he had been offered. It was the chance, he concluded, for someone else. He may also have felt a certain loyalty towards the Earl of Rowcester, whose fortunes had been temporarily restored but who would be in difficulties again as soon as the cameras left the location. It was Jeeves's great moment for decision and we must feel, surely, that he chose the better way and was essentially true to himself.

The filming came to an end and the camera crews departed, together with executives, technicians, character players and stars. The scene at Rowcester Abbey was uncannily quiet. Now engaged to marry Jill Wyvern, the Earl of Rowcester thought again of how to bolster his slender income. With Jeeves, he thumbed through the Classified Trades section of the telephone directory, but without finding inspiration. Jeeves paused a moment at the section headed 'TURF ACCOUNTANTS' but the Earl did not immediately react. Jeeves decided on the indirect approach.

'Well, my lord, my own income includes, as one element, my winnings on the turf. Has your lordship considered flat racing as a source of profit?'

'I've considered it every bally year but I lose more often than I win. The only people certain of winning – yourself apart – are the bookmakers.'

'That being so, my lord, your best policy might be to set up in business as a bookmaker.'

'Me? Impossible, Jeeves. Inheriting a title of nobility has its drawbacks. I can't sit in the House of Commons for example. Nor can I practise as a bookie. A pity, Jeeves, but there it is. It's simply not on.'

'I realize your difficulty, my lord. You would have to adopt a suitable name and disguise.'

'I see what you mean. But I should need a bookie's clerk and one who knows the business.'

'I should be prepared to assist your lordship in that capacity.'

'Also in disguise?' (Jeeves nodded) 'By George, that's a sporting offer, Jeeves. We'd share the profits fifty-fifty what? A false moustache, a patch over the eye – yes, that would do it – and a loud check jacket. Now, what name should we choose?'

'How about "Honest Patch Perkins" my lord?'
'Spot on!'

At this point a pause in the narrative is indicated. We have to ask ourselves how the judicious and well informed Jeeves could have accepted – no, more, could actually have proposed – so wild a project. To have entered the service of Lord Rowcester had been a mistake in the first place. To have engineered the film shooting episode had been good-natured and loyal, but this new idea was hare-brained and untypical of Jeeves. It reflected, of course, his life-long interest in the turf but it also showed, perhaps, a certain affection for Jill Wyvern whose early marriage might otherwise have been in doubt. Suffice it to say that the plan was agreed, the items of disguise were acquired and Honest Patch Perkins made his first appearance at Newmarket in April, having an extremely successful day. Encouraged by this result, the Earl had one of two rooms redecorated and even paid his tailor's bill. He did quite well at several of the lesser race meetings, although on a smaller scale. What could he do now on the St Leger? In three days at Doncaster he actually made four hundred and twenty pounds. Then came the Oaks and with it, disaster. A filly called Whistler's Mother won by a couple of lengths at thirty-three to one and a tough looking character called Captain Biggar won the double on her. Lord Rowcester had failed to lay off Biggar's second wager and lacked the money to pay up. There was nothing else for it – he and Jeeves sprinted out of the enclosure, ran to their car and drove off at speed, closely pursued, however, by Captain Biggar, to whom the Earl owed over three thousand pounds. It had been Rowcester's intention to make good his loss on the Derby but this was now out of the question because he dared not show his false moustache there again. His career as a bookmaker was over and his financial position was worse than ever. The critical situation reached its peak when Captain Biggar appeared at Rowcester, having taken the number of the Earl's numberplate, and asked how it came about that the Earl should apparently have lent his car to a welshing bookmaker.

The situation was saved by what we might describe as a really remarkable coincidence. A widowed millionairess called Mrs Spottsworth appeared and fell in love with Rowcester Abbey (ghosts and all) and it also appeared that Captain Biggar, the big game hunter, had for years been in love with her. The situation did not resolve itself immediately but all was well in the end. The last difficulty to be overcome lay in the fact that the Abbey, although everything that Mrs Spottsworth had ever dreamt about, was extremely damp, and she was, alas, a victim of fibrositis and sciatica. She was about to cancel the deal when Jeeves intervened:

'I wonder if I might make a suggestion, madam, which I think should be satisfactory to all parties.'

'What's that?'

'Buy the house, madam, take it down stone by stone and ship it to California.'

'And put it up there?' Mrs Spottsworth beamed.

'Why, what a brilliant idea!'

'Thank you, madam,'

The idea derived, in fact, from William Randolph Hearst, who could never resist any castle or abbey he happened to notice. When he died there was a whole abbey at San Simeon which had not even been unpacked. Jeeves had never been there but he had apparently visited St Donat Castle in Wales to which Mr Hearst had added features from elsewhere (castles, churches and so on), with very interesting results. Some would question whether Rowcester Abbey would be quite the same thing when re-erected in the Californian sunlight. Wouldn't something of the atmosphere be lost? It would seem not improbable, but maybe they could ship the atmosphere as well? Modern technology can achieve almost anything.

With the great moment when the Earl of Rowcester was saved, having the funds at last for the pedigree herd he really wanted, Jeeves tactfully gave notice, explaining that Bertie Wooster needed him, which at the moment was true. But Jeeves, who now saw himself more as a butler than a valet, had come to a firm decision on one point. If he was to be a butler again it must be with an employer who possessed considerable wealth. His adventures with impoverished noblemen like Lord Chuffnell and the Earl of Rowcester might make a good story or two for future gossip but lacked the element of permanence. A proper buttling career demands, he saw, a background of solid wealth; just such a background as he had known years ago when valet to Lord Worplesdon. Since then, Lord Worplesdon had married the wealthy Mrs Gregson, Bertie Wooster's formidable Aunt Agatha. Together, they must be very prosperous indeed. It is true that a wealthy bachelor would have been preferable but how few of them kept the sort of establishment in which a butler could serve with dignity! It is true again that Mr Wooster dreaded the wrath of Aunt Agatha, but butlers are not as vulnerable as nephews. He decided to make inquiries. There had been some rumour of an impending vacancy at Steeple Bumpleigh Hall. He would call in at the Junior Ganymede and ask for the latest news. It would be an odd circumtance to go full circle, as it were, and end with Lord W. again. There would be drawbacks, as he could well imagine, but he could do worse. With Lord W. he shared at least an interest in the turf. Here was a possibility that he should not ignore.

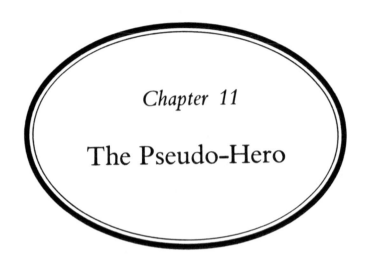

Chapter 11

The Pseudo-Hero

The Earl and Countess of Worplesdon were always down to breakfast at nine and would sit at either end of a fairly long mahogany table at which their guests, if any, would sit on either side. On the June morning which was to open a new and significant phase in Jeeves's life there were no guests present. The Earl and Countess, both a little deaf, shouted to each other down the length of the table and Jeeves, pouring their coffee and fetching the toast, would have preferred them to send each other notes to be delivered by hand. He found it all a bit noisy and had no reason to expect that he would hear anything of interest. His pessimism on that score was to prove, however, unjustified, for Lord Worplesdon, looking up from his copy of *The Times* suddenly announced that the old Earl of Yaxley had died at his home in the West Indies.

'What was that, dear?' asked the Countess at the top of her powerful voice.

'Yaxley – dead!' shouted his lordship.

'Oh,' said the Countess without any excessive display of grief. 'Do we have to attend the funeral?'

'No – he died and was buried in Bermuda.'

'Where, dear?'

'BERMUDA!'

'I see, Percival. You needn't shout. I can hear you perfectly well so long as you speak clearly.'

'So George inherits the title,' concluded Lord Worplesdon, going back to the obituary.

The Countess, otherwise known as Aunt Agatha, absorbed this piece of news and began to ponder on its implications. Sir George Wooster, Bart. that dissolute old bachelor, that former patron of now long dead chorus girls, that disgrace to the family, would now inherit Wooster Castle and estate, not far from Market Blanding. Would the acquisition of that and the title transform him into a respectable member of society, a credit to his kith and kin? She doubted whether it would do anything of the sort but there was perhaps a chance that it might lead to his marriage and the eventual provision of a direct heir to the earldom.

Pursuing this train of thought she began to contemplate, as she had so often done over the last few years, the bachelor status of Bertram Wooster. She had taken the matter lightly at first, being prepared to pass it off with a merry laugh. Bertie had seemed no more than an overgrown schoolboy, eternal member of the fifth form. Schoolboyish he might indeed remain but Bertie was now middle-aged. There was some danger of his becoming another George, less dissolute perhaps but quite as useless. She remembered, with a shudder, the occasion when she had urged him to woo a seemingly nice girl at Cannes who turned out to be a gangster's moll. This incident had for years prevented her from mentioning the subject. Had she done so, Bertie would certainly have replied, 'That reminds me . . .'

So she would, even now, have to move indirectly and with caution. But she had already picked her candidate and not without considerable thought. For Bertie the best bride still available was Valerie Pendlebury-Davenport, sister of Bertie's friend Horace and niece of the Duke of Dunstable.* The girl must be twenty-five by now, and Aunt Agatha could not understand why she was not already married. She was not spectacularly beautiful but she was a nice girl, reasonably good looking and endowed, besides, with private means. Yes, Valerie would be very suitable indeed.

'Percy,' she called out, 'I think we shoud have Valerie to stay.'

'What's that?' asked Percival, cupping his starboard ear.

'VALERIE – we must have her to stay.' This message, fortissimo, seemed to register with the Earl who nodded and returned to his newspaper.

After a pause he looked up again and asked 'Why?'

'She might do for Bertie,' replied the Countess. Her husband nodded again in agreement if not with enthusiasm.

'I'll ask Bertie, of course, and a young couple, perhaps the Knox–Bentleys, to make up more of a party, enough for tennis or bridge.'

This time her husband barely grunted but without disagreement. Aunt Agatha began to make her plans accordingly. She would begin with a telephone call to Valerie's mother, Daphne.

At this point a digression is inevitable. It was characteristic of Aunt Agatha to discuss this little plot without

---

* The Duke of Dunstable, descended from an illegitimate son of George IV, had a consdiderable estate in Sussex and Chelsea. Valerie was thus well-connected but her fortune was inherited from her mother and had something to do with boots, toothpaste or textiles, and possibly all three.

reference to Jeeves, who was hovering within earshot. As a matter of domestic protocol there was no reason why she should. Butlers are seldom consulted about such matters, nor are they expected to offer an opinion. But Jeeves, remember, had been Bertie's adviser for years. Had this Valerie project been mooted by Bertie himself there would have been a conversation on these lines, constructed on the basis of man-to-man, adviser and advised, and Jeeves would have played his part with impeccable manners and considerable insight:

Wooster: 'I think you should know, Jeeves, that I have seen a great deal recently of Miss Valerie Pendlebury-Davenport.'

Jeeves: 'Indeed, sir?'

Wooster: 'And I don't mind telling you that she is a pipterino.'

Jeeves: 'I am sure, sir, that she has often been so described. Perhaps the feminine form, pipterina, would be more correct.'

Wooster: 'Well, she'll be at the dance this evening and I mean to pop the question.'

Jeeves: 'I beg leave to doubt, sir, whether that would be a judicious policy.'

Wooster: 'What d'you mean, Jeeves?'

Jeeves: 'I would submit, sir, that the young lady in question would be an unsuitable wife for a gentleman of your character and temperament.'

Wooster: 'You are talking through your hat.'

Jeeves: 'Shakespeare once wrote of a lady:
"she hath more hair than wit, and more faults than hairs, and more wealth than faults."'

Wooster: 'He wrote that did he?'

Jeeves: 'Yes, sir. In *Two Gentlemen of Verona,* Act III Scene I. The description might almost apply to Miss Pendlebury-Davenport.'

Wooster: 'What bally nonsense! What unutterable drivel! Valerie is an angel!'

Jeeves: 'No doubt, sir. But she is, I should have thought, an angel of rather limited intelligence and one somewhat lacking in vitality. I could not advise you to make her a proposal, sir, and the less so in that I am persuaded that she would promptly accept.'

Wooster: 'I never heard such rot.'

Jeeves: 'Very good, sir.'

Where Bertie was concerned, that was the sort of discussion which Jeeves expected, ending when Bertie realized that Jeeves had been right. As we know, Jeeves was opposed to Bertie marrying anyone, which takes something from the value of his opinion. The point, however, is that Jeeves expected that people would ask his advice. Aunt Agatha did not realize what hostility she aroused merely by ignoring him. He was not at all used to being ignored, and did not like it at all.

Aunt Agatha, to whom we must now return, was busy with her plans and notably, at the outset, with her telephone call to Valerie's mother.

'It would be a great pleasure,' she explained, 'to have Valerie as our guest, should she be free to come. There will be other young guests and my nephew Bertie will be one of them. Between ourselves, I think that he should end this bachelor existence and settle down.'

'Well, Agatha,' said Daphne, 'I feel the same way about Valerie. She has been my despair, having had many proposals, some quite eligible, and having so far refused them all. I am sometimes quite vexed with her!'

'But why is she so hard to please?'

'Her trouble is that she reads too many romantic novels. She expects to marry a hero, someone just returned from battle with a bullet hole through his hat and blood on his sword.'

'But surely that is a little unreasonable in peacetime? There are plenty of army officers, for that matter, and some in the cavalry.'

'Yes, Agatha, but they only talk about cricket and tennis. Her attitude is quite ridiculous and I tell her so but she is obstinate too. Anyway, she is free to come and will accept, I'm sure. I should only like to think that something would come of it.'

The small house party was arranged, Bertie accepting with obvious reluctance, and Aunt Agatha was left to wonder by what alchemy she could turn Bertie into a hero. What qualities did he need? Jeeves, had he been consulted, would have been ready with a quotation from *Troilus and Cressida*, 'Is not birth, beauty, good shape, discourse, manhood, learning, gentleness, virtue, youth, liberality and such like, the spice and salt that season a man?' Too right, but did such a description apply to Bertie Wooster? Aunt Agatha would have had to concede that it did not. She had to admit, to begin with, that he was unheroic in appearance.

One of Bertie's more perceptive girl friends, Pauline Stoker, once said to him, 'There is a sort of woolly-headed duckiness about you,' and she was right. But duckiness is almost the opposite of heroism. It would be of no great help in quelling a mutiny or shooting a rhinoceros. That Bertram had very real virtues is certain, as for example in his determination to help his friends, but it would be difficult to present him as the superman of Valerie's dreams. Seeing his limitations, Aunt Agatha swore to succeed in spite of them. She had never, throughout her life, had troops worthy of her leadership but she knew by now how to make do with the men she had. By the time her guests had assembled, her plan had been drawn up and all with a part to play had been suitably briefed.

The dining-room at Steeple Bumpleigh Hall opened

through french windows on a well-kept lawn beyond which was a belt of trees, part of a wood in which pheasants were preserved. Walking along the edge of this wooded area on an afternoon when Valerie was absorbed in a recently acquired novel called *With Cloak and Rapier*, Bertram was accosted by the old gardener who showed him a snare he had just found in the wood. 'Lookee, zir, there are some varmints of lads who are after rabbits and maybe after pheasants as well. I'm not here after five of an evening but you might care to keep your eyes open, like. They aren't proper poachers, just village boys out for mischief. If you would chase 'em off they'll not come back. They'll be here soon after dark, I reckon. Don't tell the Countess, zir, or any of the others – I don't want to frighten people, like – but seeing you are her ladyship's nephew, I thought maybe you wouldn't mind.' Bertie promised to do his best and presently joined the others for tea. There could be no foursome at tennis because Teddy Knox-Bentley had gone lame, but all joined in the less energetic game of croquet.

That evening they had reached the final stages of an indifferent dinner when, suddenly, Teddy, whose seat faced the window, called out, 'Look, there are some trespassers over there in the wood!' He hobbled over to the window, peering into the twilight, 'Yes, they must be poachers. I'm lame, curse it – will you go, Bertie?' Seeing that his cue for action had come, Bertie strode to the window. As he did so, Teddy took down a sword from the wall and handed it to him. 'This is better than nothing, old man.' The sword had belonged, by the way, to a Victorian Colonel whose only fighting had been against his relatives.

'Thanks!' said Bertie and ran across the lawn, sword in hand. (His opponents were mere boys, after all). As he came near the edge of the wood he heard more noise than he expected. There was shouting and the clash of steel. He swiped aimlessly at the bushes and hesitated, hoping that Jeeves would join him. Then a number of shots were fired, causing him to hesitate again.

A minute later a figure emerged from the trees and turned out to be the gardener, who said, 'Well done, Mr Wooster, you gave 'em a good scare – you with your sword an' all!' The old man felt the sword blade with his glove and added, 'Not too sharp, though!'

Concluding that the battle was over, Bertie said goodnight to the gardener and walked back to the french windows. 'Well done, Bertie!' said Teddy.

'Well done!' said the others.

And then Aunt Agatha cried, 'For heaven's sake, there's blood on his sword!' So there was, as all could see and Bertie was, despite himself, the hero of the hour.

Valerie looked at him with tears in her eyes: 'But, Bertie,' she cried, 'You might have been killed!'

'It was nothing,' he replied modestly. 'It was nothing at all!'

By next day Aunt Agatha could see that her plan had been a complete success. Valerie looked at her superman with a devotion which none could mistake. We are all susceptible to flattery and Bertram had no rooted objection to hero worship. What was that quotation he had been reminded of: 'She lov'd me for the dangers I had pass'd; and I lov'd her that she did pity them.'? The lines seemed jolly appropriate and all that. What worried him however was the general assumption that he and Valerie would want to be left alone. He liked the girl and he was happy to have her as a partner at tennis after Teddy's lameness had disappeared, which it did almost at once. He did not mind going for walks with her and he was ready, on occasion, to hold her hand. As against that, he had no intention of marrying her, partly because he was not in love and partly because he could not pose for ever as a man of exceptional courage. She would expect to see him perform feats of daring at regular intervals, renewing her faith in his intrepid character, but this was not a role he could maintain. To marry her under false pretences would have been most unfair, even had she been his dream girl in other respects. But how could he look into her admiring eyes and say 'Sorry, it's not on.' He felt somehow trapped and decided that he must ask Jeeves for his advice.

Having lost Jeeves as a valet he was lucky indeed to be staying in a household where Jeeves was now the butler. He found an opportunity to visit Jeeves in the butler's pantry and said quietly, after glancing guiltily round, 'Look, Jeeves, I'm in a fix.'

To which that admirable man responded at once, 'So I've noticed, sir. Your aunt set it up but I can assure you that I was no party to it.'

'But, Jeeves, what am I to *do*?'

'There is only one answer, sir. We must stage another scene in which you appear in a different light. You need to reveal yourself, sir, as a laggard in love and a dastard* in war.'

'As a what in what?'

'As a dastard in war. I quote, sir, from *Marmion* by Sir Walter Scott. Once you have shown cowardice, Miss Pendlebury-Davenport will lose interest in you, sir, and you can make your escape.' There can be no doubt that Jeeves knew exactly what to do, nor need we question that he was glad to plan the rescue, but we may also

---

* The word 'dastard' is no longer in frequent use, although the adjective 'dastardly' is readily attached to any crime or brutal act in which the criminal runs no personal risk himself. The word was new to Bertram and it was never to be a part of his rather limited vocabulary. It may be doubted, in fact, whether he and Sir Walter Scott had very much in common.

suspect that his scheme reflected a desire to thwart Aunt Agatha. The Countess was someone for whom he now felt an intense dislike.

'If, I might be allowed to make the suggestion, I think, sir, that you should take Miss Pendlebury-Davenport for a walk on Tuesday afternoon.'

'Why Tuesday, Jeeves?'

'That, sir, is my afternoon off. I suggest that you take the path which leads from the Red Lion towards the village of Much Middlefold. It is quite a pleasant walk, sir, and leads you to the picturesque watermill, often a subject for sketching in watercolour or crayon. To view this would be a reasonable object for the afternoon's exertion.'

'Yes, Jeeves – and what then?'

'Somewhere in that vicinity you may be intercepted by a dangerous looking tramp who will demand your wallet while threatening you with some suitably blunt instrument. I suggest that you reveal your craven* character and hand the wallet over. It is a simple plot just such as Shakespeare describes in *Midsummer Night's Dream*:

> "*A play there is, my lord, some ten words long,*
> *Which is as brief as I have known a play:*
> *But, by ten words, my lord, it is too long.*"

It will be enough, however, to serve our purpose. Following this incident Miss Pendlebury-Davenport will transfer her affection to some other gentleman;

*It was typical of Jeeves to use the word 'craven' in a context where the author or reader would have used the alternative word 'pusillanimous'. In the mediaeval Ordeal by Battle the protagonist who was fairly back against the ropes would cry 'Craven' and be judged the loser. The name was given to an area of Yorkshire in which (we presume) no local character had ever been known to win.

perhaps a big-game hunter who has recently been on safari in Africa.'

'You have genius, Jeeves! There is no other word for it. Your brain, when you die, should be placed in a museum.'

'I endeavour to give satisfaction, sir.'

At breakfast on Tuesday the Earl of Worplesdon looked up from *The Times* and gave all those present a news item of family interest: 'George has married!' These tidings reached Aunt Agatha via her guests, who now provided a sort of bush telegraph.

'Who is the bride?' was the question passed back by the same means.

'Maud Wilberforce,' came the answer and Aunt Agatha speculated as to whether she could be a member of the Essex or Oxfordshire branch of that family. When these doubts and queries were conveyed to the Earl, he settled the question through having prior knowledge of the lady concerned.

'Maudie,' he said firmly, 'was a buxom barmaid at the Criterion when I was young – the one with orange coloured hair. She was well known in those days – the toast of the Boulevards, what? In *The Times* she is described now as a widow living at Wisteria Lodge, Kitchener Road, East Dulwich, SE.'

'How old would she be now?' asked Valerie.

'What's that? How old? At a guess, about sixty-five. I last saw her about forty years ago.'

'Jolly sporting and all that!' said Bertie.

'Sporting?' exclaimed Lord Worplesdon. 'George is out of his mind and this marriage will probably kill him. To think of Maudie becoming Countess of Yaxley! The Gaiety Girls don't have it all their own way . . .'

Aunt Agatha lapsed into a moody silence, thinking no doubt that her own title as Countess had been rather devalued. Impeccably attentive at the sideboard, Jeeves made inwardly a quick survey of the family tree, but failed to place the next heir to the Earldom, who would certainly not be a child of the present Earl and Countess. Other people started other subjects of conversation and Bertie told Valerie about the old watermill. Would she like to walk there that afternoon? It soon appeared that she would like nothing better. Bertie promised to bring his camera.

It proved a fine afternoon for a country walk, sunny but with a cool breeze. The countryside was looking its best and Bertie, helping Valerie over a style, found that her hand was still in his as they crossed the next field. The old watermill would be a highly romantic setting, as Valerie knew, and the very place at which her hero might well propose to her. She told Bertie about the book she was still reading called *With Cloak and Rapier*, 'Everard Dashwood is a penniless younger son but the best swordsman in the county. He falls in love with Mary Drummand whose only brother was killed at the Battle of Flodden. I wondered at first about the cloak mentioned in the title. I could see that he would need a cloak in cold weather but I thought that could have been taken for granted.'

'Just what I feel. Rather like "With mackintosh and rapier." That doesn't sound right, does it?'

'Well, the point is that the cloak was wrapped round the left arm, which could then be used as a shield.'

'Jolly smart idea! I wonder who first thought of that? Someone pretty brainy, I should think.'

'Well, it's an exciting story. They're terribly in love, you see. She is so pretty and he is so brave.'

'I'll bet they marry in the end. It would never do in a novel if she died of measles and he was killed in a road accident.'

'Oh, that couldn't happen! I hate a novel with a sad ending.'

On this happy note the walk, continuing, brought them to the old and picturesque watermill, no longer functioning but provided still with a millpool, a mill race and weir.

'What a lovely place!' exclaimed Valerie, clasping her hands.

'Jolly picturesque and all that!' said Bertie, unslinging the small box camera he had brought with him.

At that moment came disaster. A sinister and shabby figure came out of the bushes, evidently a tramp, whose dark face was partly hidden by a dirty scarf and whose hat was pulled down over his eyes. In his right hand the tramp carried a rusty iron bar.

'C'mn, mister,' he growled. 'You'd like to give a poor man a hand! What's a pound to you? To me it's food and shelter. C'mn, hand it over, guv. Or maybe you'd rather 'ave a crack over the 'ead with this?'

'Go away at once!' replied Bertie. 'Go away or I'll call the police.'

'Ow'll you do that, Guv? You scream for 'elp and I'll crack your girl over the 'ead as well!'

'Oh, Bertie!' wailed Valerie. 'Do something!'

'Look here, my man,' said Bertie, 'I ought to have you arrested but I'll help you this once. I'll give you a pound and then you'll go away quietly – eh?' Bertie took out his wallet, which the tramp promptly snatched from him.

'And nah I want 'er purse as well!' The tramp flourished his weapon and Bertie's courage seemed to ooze away.

'Look Valerie – you'd better give it him!'

Valerie gave Bertie a look of scorn, and then opened her handbag and took out the purse.

'There – take it!' she hissed and, to Bertie, 'You utter coward! You miserable weakling! To think that I regarded you as a hero – you, the man who is afraid of this dirty old tramp!'

The tramp pocketed the wallet and purse and disappeared again with a growling threat of what he would do to them if they told the police.

'How disgraceful!' exclaimed Bertie. 'What are things coming to, with daylight robbery! Let's hurry to the police station at Much Middlefold. We'll have this fellow in prison by nightfall. Never heard of such cheek!'

As Bertie uttered these protests he was standing, camera in hand, on the edge of the millpool. He felt, quite suddenly, a severe blow delivered from the rear. He tottered for a moment, waving his arms and trying to regain his balance. He failed and went into the pool with a splash. It took him a full minute to realize that Valerie had kicked him in . . . and then had undoubtedly run off, sobbing, the way they had come. Bertie was a fair swimmer but his first efforts were misdirected. The mossy stonework round the mill offered no foothold and he finally changed his mind, swam upstream, and found a muddy place where he could come ashore. As he did so, he saw that a policeman stood opposite him, holding a bicycle and a notebook.

'What's all this? asked the constable. 'Looks like a case of attempted suicide. That's illegal and I won't 'ave it on my beat.'

'Just an accident, officer!' gasped Bertie, 'I fell in.'

'What was you a doing 'ere anyway?'

'Ph-photographing the old m-m-mill.'

'Where's your camera?'

'At the bottom of the pool.'

'You'll come along to the police station, where I shall have some questions to ask. Come on, now – and don't you try to commit suicide again!'

Before the situation could deteriorate any further a third figure appeared on the scene. It was Jeeves, immaculate in morning coat and bowler hat, who now intervened with smooth efficiency.

'Excuse me, officer. I can answer for this gentleman. I am butler to the Rt. Hon. the Earl of Worplesdon. Mr Wooster here is one of his lordship's guests. I have come to fetch him with a car which is parked in the village.' There was little more to be said and the incident came to an end. The car, Bertie's own sports model, contained a bath towel, an immediate change of clothes, and the luggage which Bertie had brought with him for the visit.

'If we drive back at once to the Hall, sir, we should be there before Miss Pendlebury-Davenport returns. I suggest, sir, that you leave me at the lodge gates and drive straight on to the railway station at Steeple Bumpleigh. There is a train to London at 4.25. I shall explain to the Earl and Countess that you had an urgent telephone call, your affairs making it imperative that you should go to London immediately. I shall convey your thanks for their very kind hospitality and assure them that you will be writing as soon as you have the opportunity.'

'But how will you deal with Miss Pendlebury-Davenport? She will be telephoning the police!'

'I shall tell her that the miscreant has already been arrested on a more serious charge, and will prove this by returning her purse. I shall urge her to say nothing about her recent adventure, pointing out the extreme inconvenience of having to appear as a witness.'

'Jeeves, you have thought of everything. Or *nearly* everything . . .'

'What have I forgotten, sir?'

'You have forgotten to return me my wallet. As you do so, however, please retain ten pounds as a small recompense for your help on this occasion.'

'Thank you very much, sir,' replied Jeeves as he returned the wallet. 'I endeavour to give satisfaction.'

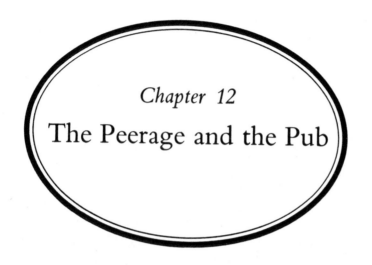

Chapter 12

The Peerage and the Pub

In a purely technical sense, Jeeves's work as a butler was beyond criticism. The fact remains, however, that his heart was not in it. Had Aunt Agatha died (she who would plainly live for ever) Jeeves could have been content to serve Lord Worplesdon for years. He might be irritable and he was certainly deaf but Jeeves had established with him a good working relationship. He had been wrong in thinking that he could do the same with the Countess. Nor were things improved by the episode which ended the potential romance between Valerie and Bertram. There was something fishy about the whole incident, some counter-plot of which she could never discover the truth. Bertie would have married years ago had it not been for Jeeves, and she felt that Jeeves had once again spoilt everything. In one respect at least Jeeves had been right to join the Worplesdon menage; they were people with money enough and to spare. There were other drawbacks, however, and there were moments when Jeeves looked back with nostalgia to his service with noblemen who had been utterly broke. He gradually came to the conclusion that his days as a domestic servant were coming to an end. Should he retire? He had by now a modest independence but the prospect of life in retirement did not attract him. He wanted still to exercise his talents but in some rather different field – he did not know what. He went about polishing the silver with a dwindling enthusiasm and a growing dislike of the Countess, whose dislike for him was certainly no less.

The crisis came one evening when the Worplesdons were dining alone. The Countess mentioned casually, yet of course loudly, that the committee had all but agreed on their candidate for the constituency at the coming by-election (caused by the sitting member's unfortunate demise).

'There were a dozen applicants to consider but the majority considered that the one I recommended would be the best.'

'I am sure you did, my dear. What name did you put forward?'

'Mr Aubrey Upjohn. He was considered some years ago at Market Snodbury but was finally turned down.'

'Upjohn? Upjohn? Wasn't he the headmaster of a prep. school at Bramley-on-sea – the one attended by Bertie and by many of his friends?'

'Mr Upjohn was indeed headmaster of Malvern House. Since those days he has inherited a fortune from his uncle and this has enabled him to go in for politics.'

'I remember now. Upjohn, to be sure. Not that I particularly liked the chap.'

'I don't like him either. I think, however, that he is capable of winning the by-election. That was my opinion, and the other committee members agreed with me.'

Lord Worplesdon could well believe her. The committee which dared disagree with Agatha had still to be formed. He felt vaguely resentful, knowing that Upjohn would inevitably dine with them in the near future. He privately thought the man a pompous ass. He supposed, however, that this was a basic qualification for the House of Commons. He moodily had some Stilton, stood up while his wife withdrew, drank his usual glass of port and presently rejoined Agatha in the drawing room. She poured him a cup of coffee and he helped himself to cream and sugar.

At that point their evening routine was interrupted. Jeeves, who should have withdrawn at this point, was still in the room. It appeared, moreover, that he had something to say.

'Lord and Lady Worplesdon, I hope I may be pardoned for taking the liberty . . . I could not help overhearing the news about Mr Aubrey Upjohn. I wish to submit, with all due respect, that his selection as candidate would be most inadvisable.'

Lady Worplesdon was unused to receiving advice from her servants or even from her relatives. Her cold stare of surprise lowered the temperature of the room by about two degrees. It was her husband, however, who broke the tense silence which had ensued.

'Why inadvisable, eh?'

'Mr Upjohn was not a success, my lord, at Market Snodbury. I was present at the time when his adoption as candidate was under discussion. Apart, however, from his mediocre performances as a speaker, he has many active opponents. A large number of his former pupils at Malvern House have formed a society, the members of which are sworn to thwart his political ambitions by every means in their power. It is called the Downjohn Society and its members practice the art of throwing rotten eggs; an art in which some of them have become extremely proficient. I felt, my lord, that these are facts of which your lordship should be apprised.'

At this point Lord Worplesdon would probably have thanked Jeeves and returned to the article he was reading on trade prospects in Venezuela. The Countess, by contrast, was livid with rage. She did not accept advice from servants. If she had, this would have been the last servant to whom she would have listened. As against that, she realized that Jeeves was right and that Upjohn would have to be rejected. Remembering speech days long ago at Malvern House, she realized that the old boys must be numerous and influential, and from what Bertram had said about the place, she had no doubt that he was a member of the Downjohn Society, if not indeed its founder. As one who had played racquets for Oxford, his aim with a rotten egg would be unimaginably accurate. He and his friends were all members, besides, of the Drones Club at which the members pelted each other at lunch time with crusty rolls. A by-election with Upjohn on the hustings would end with the candidate in hospital and with most of her younger relatives in jail.

There was no doubt about what she must do. She would have to convene the selection committee and tell them that she had been mistaken about Upjohn. In the light of new information he no longer had her support. But what a humiliating experience it was going to be! The idea that the Countess could be mistaken was a concept now beyond the other members. It was not a concept she wished to introduce nor could she see it as other than disastrous in its consequences. She could have avoided all this impending chaos had she merely consulted Aunt Dahlia, who could have told her all. It would be no exaggeration to say that Aunt Agatha's expression was such as might purge the soul with terror.

To digress a little, it is a commonplace that the dictators of this world, past and present, are apt to resent anything in the nature of a setback. When there has been a military defeat the Leader's staff officers do not compete with each other for the privilege of telling him about it. There takes place, as a rule, one of those competitions in reluctance, each saying, 'You tell him' to some other, who says, 'You tell him' in turn to someone more junior. The point is reached when the most junior present, usually holding the rank of major, looking desperately around for a captain and seeing none, comes to realize that the task will inevitably be his. The result, as all had foreseen, is that the bearer of ill tidings is reduced to the ranks for disloyalty. In the circumstances he may be thought to have got off lightly. Now, Aunt Agatha, the unquestioned dictator of Southmolton-shire, shared many characteristics with other and better known dictators. The sensation of being thwarted, a rare event, was apt to leave her in an ugly mood. That mood she now made public in words she had chosen with vindictive care: 'Jeeves, when we wish for your political advice, we shall be sure to ask for it. In the ordinary way a butler is not required to play any very conspicuous part in a by-election. In the choice of a parliamentary candidate I do not expect my domestic servants to have any knowledge or voice any opinion. I am happier, indeed, if they will confine themselves to the work for which they are paid. And so, Jeeves, I must ask you, in future, to keep your views to yourself and leave political problems to those who are better informed. I hope I make myself clear?'

'Quite clear, your ladyship. I entirely understand your point of view and am only sorry that my attempt to assist you was so unwelcome. In the circumstances you will be neither surprised nor sorry when I give you a month's notice as from to-day. I hope my successor will better know his place.'

Far from Steeple Bumpleigh and knowing nothing of the clash of personalities that had taken place there, Bertie Wooster was once more in his London flat and without a valet. He had recently arrived back from his eventful stay with the Worplesdons and Jeeves's resignation was still an event of the future. The flat was cleaned by a charwoman and he had all his meals out. Too many of his friends were out of town and he was rather pleased than otherwise when he received a telephone call from Kipper Herring, perhaps his oldest friend and one he had not seen for three weeks. Kipper wanted to come and see him and Bertie told him to come round straight away. Given an armchair and a beer, Kipper came straight to the point: 'I wanted you to know before anyone else. Bobbie and I have broken off our engagement. We had a long talk yesterday and decided to call it off.'

'Good grief – what did you quarrel about?'

'That's just it – we didn't quarrel. We are still the best of friends but we have found that, in practice, we don't like the same sort of life. I am a working journalist, an Assistant Editor, more or less tied to London. Bobbie is really a country girl. She can take London in small doses but she doesn't want to spend her life there. She is bored with my friends – they are all too bookish for her. And then there's her mother . . .'

'A very interesting person and a novelist.'

'Yes, yes, I know that. But she had always assumed that Bobbie would marry into the nobility or at least marry a member of the cabinet. She thinks me inadequate and makes that obvious whenever we meet.'

'I know, Kipper, I know exactly what you mean. She thought me inadequate too. She did not say so, not in so many words, but one could read between the lines.'

'Exactly. One has a sixth sense. She can't see me as the

right husband for Bobbie and I have begun to see that she is right.'

'But I wouldn't say that, Kipper. That young hell-raiser, that maker of apple-pie beds, that red-headed menace needs a firm hand. She needs more than that, she needs a good spanking. Well, you are clearly the man; you with your reputation as a boxer, as tough a chap as one can see around.'

'I thought that once, Bertie, but it doesn't seem to work out. So it's all over and I thought you should know.'

'Could I do anything to help, old man? What if I talked to her and tried to mediate?'

'No good, Bertie. You can mediate when there has been a quarrel. You can't mediate where the two people concerned are actually agreed.'

'I suppose you're right. Have some more beer?'

'Thanks . . . I felt I had to get away from her to think things over, so I went to stay at an old inn called the Anglers' Rest, near Market Blandings in Shropshire.'

'I didn't know you were keen on fishing?'

'With a name like mine? How could I be? But I think best on a river bank and I like the Anglers' Rest – one of the best places of its sort. The landlord, they tell me, is just about to retire. I do hope his successor won't spoil the place in making another road house. Anyway, I spent a long weekend there and thought it out. "It's no good," I told myself. Then I had it out with Bobbie. It was sad at the time but I know that we've done the right thing.'

'Have some more beer.'

'Thanks. Anyway, I recommend the Anglers' Rest as a quiet place in which to think.'

'I've made a note of it already. I know the place by sight but have never stopped there.'

'I feel shattered,' groaned Kipper, 'and yet, somehow, relieved.'

'I know. I felt like that when Pauline Stoker broke off our engagement. The fact is, I was jolly glad. Now what about this evening? Shall we dine somewhere and go to a show?'

'Jolly nice of you to suggest it, but I have a date with a very sympathetic girl who is sub-editor of a Woman's Magazine. I expect I shall cry on her shoulder. It's nothing serious, of course. We are mere friends who happen to be in the same line of business.'

'Of course, of course. Well, you'll want to be on your way. All the best, old man, and if Bobbie wants a shoulder to cry on, I shall be glad to offer her mine.'

That last thought remained with Bertie and he decided to send Bobbie an end-of-engagement present. It was easier to decide on the policy than conclude what the present should be. Jeeves would have suggested a book on philosophy – Spinoza's latest or the sayings of Marcus Aurelius. Bertie did not pursue that idea but he went next morning to Harridge's, looking for inspiration. He did not find it or, anyway, not immediately. The trouble with Harridge's is that its mere vastness is a discouragement in itself. Enter the place with a clear idea of what you want and there is some likelihood of your emerging with the thing under your arm, whether a bottle of Tokay, a Ming vase, a treacle-cured ham or a neutered Poodle that has already had distemper. Enter the place, as Bertie did, with the idea of buying a present for Roberta Wickham and the problem looms immense. You might end by buying anything from a cigarette lighter to a Persian rug. Aimless at first, Bertie ended up in a department which sold, among other things, the sort of address book which is bound in calf and stamped in gold with the arms of Louis XIV. It would hint to her delicately that she would have other telephone numbers to note in the years to come. He looked at several of these in turn, rejecting one as too big, another as too ornate, and he was just finalizing his choice when he noticed a girl approaching the same section of the store from the other direction. She was copper-haired, shapely, and extremely pretty . . . Could it be? It was! It was Roberta Wickham and she was almost certainly looking for an end–of–engagement present for Kipper. It had seemed to her, no doubt, that an address book, a rather sumptuous one, would hint, delicately of course, that there were other pebbles on the whatsit or birds, did he mean, in the bush? She blushed when she saw Bertie and then kissed him rather quickly. 'You know about Reggie and I?'

He nodded and then answered, 'That's why I'm here. I wanted to give you a present.'

'And I was finding a present for Reggie? How sweet of you to think of me, though!'

'Do you like it?'

'I love it. Do you think Reggie will like this?'

'Bound to, I should say. Funny thing, though, our meeting like this . . .'

At this point we must again digress because some reader might say at this point that this is too much of a coincidence. That they should have the same idea we might accept, but not, surely, at the same hour on the same day! What the reader forgets is that he is reading a biography, not a mere work of fiction. This is what happened. And why should it seem so unlikely? There is a certain unconscious telepathy between people who are fond of each other. They do gravitate towards the same spot, without any deliberate purpose, and they are each surprised to find the other there. It happens all the time, it does really.

And, as on many another such occasion, it ended inevitably in their having lunch together. Looking across the table in Harridge's restaurant, Bobbie's eyes were bright with tears as she told Bertie about her parting with Reggie. He realized, as he listened, that Bobbie was growing up. She hated to think that she could have made anyone unhappy. He found it difficult to believe that he had ever thought her a menace to society. It was soon arranged that he should take her out to dinner on the following evening. It transpired that she had never been to Beachcombers, so that was evidently the place to dine and dance.

It should be explained at this point that Beachcombers is a place with a Polynesian atmosphere and is a shade more Polynesian than are the South Sea Islands themselves. Where you have your preliminary drink, a concoction of fruit juice and rum, you have beside you a moving cloud effect and the sound of thunder is heard in the distance. A waterfall splashes into a pool containing real turtles. You are, for all practical purposes, an Outcast of the Islands, with Somerset Maugham at the next table and Joseph Conrad at the table beyond. Bobbie was enchanted and looked enchanting. Nobody's shoulders were ever so white, nobody's hands were ever so delicate, nobody else was as stunningly pretty. After more drinks they went into the restaurant where the decor and the menu were not quite consistent with the effect achieved in the bar. The management had not wanted to seem pedantic. The influences at work varied, therefore, from Canton to Bali, from Tahiti to Ceylon. The general effect was vaguely exotic and it was certainly a place to have fun. They had a Chinese Malayan dinner, they danced to a Philippino band and presently, when the musicians rested, they were able to talk.

'You know, Bobbie, I have always loved you. But you were such a danger to the public that I was half afraid of you. Why were you such a horror, darling?'

'Well, I thought you might have guessed. I am an only

child and my father wanted a boy – hence the name. I became a tom-boy to please him. He died when I was aged seven and mother took to writing novels, with precious little time for me. I am very affectionate – well, you know that – but I had rather a rotten time in my young days, chiefly loving my pony and my dog. So I went rather wild when I had the chance. I'll tell you something, Bertie, which may help you to understand. There was a moment – do you remember? – when I had to choose, or thought I had to choose, between you and Reggie. I chose Reggie and explained to you, "I can't marry everybody."'

'Yes, darling, I remember.'

'Well, I did feel like that at the time. I loved you both and had love to spare for a dozen more. I am more prepared now to settle for one.'

'Would you settle for me, Bobbie?'

'Yes, Bertie, but don't you see the difficulty? Mother wants me to marry someone with a title – a baron at the very least. Father was only a baronet, something she always resented. So mother will be awfully difficult about this. She rather dislikes you anyway.'

'She does indeed. But can't we tell her where she gets off?'

'But, darling, I do hate making anyone unhappy. I wouldn't hurt her for anything – I really couldn't, not for the world.'

'And that is one of the nicest things about you . . .'

'You do understand? . . . You kiss rather nicely.'

'I need more practice to regain my mid-season form.'

'All right, darling – but let's dance!'

It was a wonderful evening but it ended on the same uncertain note. They loved each other but Lady Wickham stood between them. Bertie talked bravely about persuading her to see reason but Bobbie, looking dubious, would only shake her head.

Arriving home, long after midnight, at his empty flat – and it seemed more empty than he had ever seen it – Bertie picked up the evening paper which had been thrust through the letterbox at some earlier hour. Quite automatically he glanced at the pages, but was suddenly brought up short by a paragraph headed:

DEATH OF THE EARL OF YAXLEY

Better known as Sir George Wooster, Bart., and a well-known figure in the west end, the Earl of Yaxley, who only recently inherited the title, died early this morning at his flat off Dover Street. A bachelor for most of his life and a loyal patron of the night-clubs, the Earl finally married Maud Wilberforce, whom he first knew as a popular barmaid at the Criterion. The Earl represented an Edwardian type, the stage-door johnny or man-about-town. He was never adjusted to the less colourful age into which he had survived. He will long be remembered at Boodle's and the Devonshire, at the Café de Paris and the Café Royal. It is understood that the Countess will now return to her previous home in East Dulwich . . .

Bertie read no further but went to bed with kindly thoughts of old George, his uncle. The old boy must have been a bit lonely in his last years, having survived some of his nephews – Basil, for example, another bachelor, and Rupert who died childless (or *had* he been childless?) in Malaya. The Earldom had been of no use to the old rake, who never so much as visited the family estate, or so he had heard . . . Bertie slept late next morning and was woken by the telephone. Not Aunt Agatha, he groaned to himself. But it was neither she nor any other aunt. It was Mr Barrow of Messrs Hadley, Garrett & Stott, Solicitors, of Lincoln's Inn.

'Mr Bertram Wooster? You will have heard the sad news of the death of the 8th Earl of Yaxley? You have? Well, you may not have realized that you are now the heir to the family estate, Wooster Castle, and the Earldom itself. There have been several recent deaths in the family and you now stand in line to succeed as the 9th Earl. Would it be convenient for you to call at our office in the course of the day . . .?'

Bertie made the appointment, hung up, and gazed into the future. He was now to live a very different life, as landowner, as peer, as justice of the peace. His days for stealing policemen's helmets were definitely at an end. He rang up Bobbie Wickham.

'That you, darling? Would you care to make a telephone call to your mother? Ask her whether she approves your engagement to the 9th Earl of Yaxley? No, I'm not off my head . . . No, I am not suggesting – and anyway I couldn't – he's dead. The point is that I've just inherited the family estates and title . . . That's right, darling . . . Now call your mother and obtain her approval . . . No, you needn't tell her that it's me. She can find out from the newspaper . . . Yes, isn't it wonderful? . . . I don't believe, do you, in long engagements? . . . Oh, yes, four weeks is quite long enough . . . St George's, Hanover Square . . . All right. You couldn't make it three weeks? . . . No. I see that. Yes, I quite understand . . . Meet me for lunch, sweetheart, and we'll arrange everything.'

So everything was arranged. It will not, however, be described, or not, anyway, in this book. After all, one society wedding is much like another, and the readers can picture it for themselves. After the honeymoon the 9th Earl and his Countess drove to visit his estates. He had not been to Wooster Castle* for years and she had never been there at all. Bertie suspected that the Castle would be quite unfit for human habitation. He had accordingly booked accommodation at the Anglers' Rest, so highly recommended by Reggie. It was all, they found, that their friend had said, and the dinner, though simple, was excellent. The landlord, old Mr Haynes, came to ask his lordship whether all was to his liking.

'Fine, fine . . . But I'm sorry to hear that you are on the point of retirement. After how many years? Seventeen? Well, I think you have earned what I hope will be a long and happy retirement, living not too far away. There should be a worthy successor. Who owns the place?'

'You do, my lord.'

'Good grief! Then I'll have to give the matter some serious thought.'

Over coffee Bobbie had a favour to ask and did it (as she did everything) very prettily.

'Forgive me, sweetheart, but I'm going to demand from you a very great sacrifice. When we settle down at Wooster Castle, having made some of it habitable, I really think we should do better without Jeeves.'

'But, darling, there's no chance of his being there. He has settled down as butler to Aunt Agatha.'

'No, sweetheart, he hasn't. I was on the telephone to

---

* The mediaeval castle of Yaxley from which the Sieur de Wocester had gone forth to play his part in the Agincourt campaign (Vide supra, p. 144) had been destroyed during the Civil War by a Cromwellian Colonel too obtuse to realize that the fortification was in any case obsolete. Its place had been taken by a Regency building with a mere hint of the Gothic. The part of it still habitable is the stable building where the hayloft has been converted into a cheerful flat, neglected at this time but needing little more than redecoration. The main building looks impressive from the park but is otherwise in poor repair. No other castle in Shropshire is definitely free from ghosts.

her yesterday and learnt that Jeeves has given notice. It would be natural for you to want him back but I don't think it would be a good idea.'

'I know it wouldn't. He always warned me against you – utter rubbish but still one remembers. No, it wouldn't do. I tell you what, though. I shall make him landlord of the Anglers' Rest!'

There were people who regarded Bertie as mentally negligible. As from this time, they began to see that they had been wrong. Apart from that his noble rank and lovely bride seemed to give him a new confidence. On this occasion he went straight to the telephone and put through a call to Aunt Agatha.

'Yaxley here, your faithful nephew. I hear tell that Jeeves is to quit your service. Might I have a word with him? I am able to offer him another job.'

Jeeves was presently on the line and received Bertie's offer with all his studied lack of emotion.

'I thank your lordship for the kind offer, which I am happy to accept. I shall endeavour, as hitherto, to give your lordship every satisfaction.'

The Anglers' Rest is about twelve miles from Wooster Castle and near the road which the Earl would be likely to follow on many of his normal occasions. Over the years to come he would seldom pass the old inn without calling to have a chat with his old friend. On one of the first of these casual encounters he joined the group in the bar-parlour, where there was an animated discussion in progress on the subject of motion pictures made in Hollywood.

'What I hear,' said a gin-and-tonic, 'is that likely-looking players are put on contract and have to work for years on their original salary, even after their first film has been a big success.'

'White slavery, I'd call that,' commented Miss Postlethwaite, the popular and erudite barmaid.

'Ah, but you forget that they willingly signed the contract,' objected a hearty ginger ale. 'They would be unknown then and glad to get a part of any kind.'

'True enough,' said the milk stout, 'but a generous employer would not hold a youngster to a bad bargain.'

'What do you think, Mr Mulliner?' The gin-and-tonic addressed this question to the accepted sage of the Anglers' Rest, who was thoughtfully sipping his hot Scotch and lemon.

'The question you raise,' said Mr Mulliner, 'is one of special interest to me because it is well illustrated in the early career of one of my distant relatives, Lorna Languish, once a star of the silent screen—'

'Light is also shed on this subject by experience of my own.' This unexpected intervention came in a loud and firm voice from the new landlord himself, a voice which went on inexorably:

'When I was a character actor in Hollywood, I remember the advent there of Miss Jacqueline Fitzroy—'

'—Never heard of her,' said Mr Mulliner jealously.

'Nor would anyone know of her who had not been actually playing in Hollywood at the time. Her career in motion pictures was destined to be short. Although much admired at the time and highly valued at the Perfecto Zizzbaum Studio, she became engaged to a young English gentleman called Gussie. She sought to break her contract, thoughtlessly signed when she first appeared in Hollywood, not because the terms were ungenerous, not because her film was an unexpected success – far from that, the film had not even been made – but simply because she wished to marry. She was told she could not break the terms of her contract. She must work for Mr Levitsky until the contract expired. Hearing of her plight, I pointed out to her that there was nothing in the contract to prevent her throwing tomatoes at Mr Levitsky whenever he appeared on the set. Accepting my suggestion . . .'

Mr Jeeves spoke with quiet authority, knowing how to hold his audience. No one spoke until he had finished, no one even coughed or sneezed. The only slight interruption was the sound of the outer door closing quietly behind Mr Mulliner as he went out slowly into the cold and darkness of the night.